Now Or Never

Chester Philips

Contents

Chapter 1- The Beginning

K ate

Never in my wildest dreams, did I think I would die like this. Buried alive, by the man who I thought loved me. I knew my life was not all rainbows and cotton candy, but I never thought this would be the way I left the world. I was trapped in a box, who knows how many feet under the ground. But to understand how we got here; I will have to take you back to the beginning.

Two years earlier

"Come on, Kate, let's hurry up and hit the clubs. You only turn 21 once" my best friend Tracy calls out to me. My name is Katherine Fowley, but everyone calls me Kate. Today is my 21st birthday. I wasn't planning on going out, I just wanted a quiet night in, watching movies and overeating on junk food. You see, I was raised by people who claimed to be my parents when, in fact, I was kidnapped as a baby and flown halfway across the world to be raised by these sick fucks. They tortured me and abused me in any way they could.

"I don't wanna go anywhere, Trace. Why can't we sit at home and eat junk food?" I ask Tracy. She shakes her head and scoffs. "Kate, we have been through this a thousand times before. It would help if you broke away from the past. You got away from those fuckwits, and now it is time to live" Tracy says. I shake my head and close in on myself. I know what Tracy is saying is the truth, but my confidence levels are so low that going out in public causes anxiety and panic attacks.

"Come on, girl. We will only go out for a little while. As soon as you feel an attack coming on, we will leave, I promise you" Tracy whines. I know she is just trying to make my birthday the best it can be, but I know it will all go to shit for some reason. Just like every birthday I have had. Who knows if today is my real birthday? Those fake parents could have made it up when they took me from my birth parents.

I make my way into my bedroom. I know Tracy won't give up until I am dressed and out of the front door. I hope she doesn't mind wearing jeans. I am not getting dressed up for me to only end up back at home, on the couch in my favourite pair of trackies. I quickly throw on my jeans and an old top. I chuck my hair up in a messy ponytail and slip on my old trusty converse. I walk out of the bedroom and wait for Tracy to come out of the bathroom.

"I don't fucking think so Kate. You need to wear something a little more fancy. We are going to a club, not McDonald's for a happy meal" Tracy says. She shakes her head and walks into my bedroom. "How the fuck do you not own a dress or a skirt for that matter. Fucking hell Kate, get your boney arse back in this room and help me find something else worth wearing" she yells out to me.

I drag my feet but make my way into the bedroom. Tracy is knee-deep in my clothes. "You won't find anything in there, Tracy" I tell her. "Bullshit, I won't" she exclaims. Thirty minutes later, I am now dressed in black pants and a half dressy half casual top. Tracy never did find any shoes to match my outfit, so she threw me a pair of black ballet flats. She straightened my unruly hair and has pinned the top half back. When Tracy came towards my face with eyeliner and mascara, I shrieked and closed in on myself. She knew at that point, makeup wasn't going to happen.

"Ok, let's go. Remember, I will leave as soon as you say so, but give it a try Kate. You might enjoy yourself" Tracy says as she drags me out of my apartment. Forty minutes later we are standing in line at one of the clubs this city has. I wouldn't know if it was one of the best, I don't leave my house. I work from home, do all my shopping online. I will open a window to get fresh air, occasionally. The outside world scares me. I am thankful I found Tracy when I did, though, she saved my life four years ago.

Standing in this line, I am off in my own little world until I am pushed in the back by the people standing behind us. I give a little scream, more to myself than the people around me. Tracy quickly grabs my hand and pulls me into her. She gives the people behind us a death glare. I shake my head at her, gaining her attention. She knows I am feeling uncomfortable.

We are next in line for the security to check our ID's. "Tracy, baby, it's been a while" the security guard says to her. Tracy blushes. "Sorry, Sammy boy. I have been hanging with my girl here" she says, pointing at me. This Sammy guy gives me a once over. "Is she old enough to be here?" he asks Tracy. She nods her head. "It's actually her 21st today" she tells him. "Well happy birthday young lady. Go on in. Tell the bartender drinks are on me tonight" Sammy says to us. Tracy smiles. "I'll call you later tonight" she tells him in a whisper. He winks at her, and she drags me into the club.

Fuck! The music is loud, and strobing lights only light the place up. I can already feel a headache coming on. Tracy continues dragging me until we are at the bar. She yells over the music to the bartender. Tracy is probably telling him what that Sammy guy said. She places a glass of something red in front of me. I give her a look that says' what the fuck?' Tracy smiles and tells me to drink, using her hand to her mouth.

I take my first sip, at first it tastes fruity, and then a harshness hits. I screw my face up at it. I place the glass back down on the bench and shake my head. Tracy throws her arm around my shoulder and brings her mouth to my ear. "Happy birthday gorgeous girl. But it would help if you let loose. Let the alcohol take over your feelings and emotions. Let go of the past and look towards the future. You will go places, and I will be by your side every step of the way" she yells.

I pick the glass back up and down it in one go. I need to take her advice sometimes and why not start tonight. I can already feel the alcohol taking effect in my brain. If I knew I would be drunk off one drink and forget my worries, I would have done this a long time ago. Yes, this is the first time I have had any alcoholic beverages. Tracy places another drink in front of me. "Take it slowly this time" she yells into my ear. I give her a small nod and take a small sip of the drink.

It takes me a little while to get through this second glass. Once I had finished it, Tracy grabs my hand and pulls me towards the dance floor. I watch the people around me dancing. I follow what some of the girls are doing. Dancing to this music is not something I would have ever imagined myself doing, but here I am, surprising myself.

I am letting go as Tracy told me to. I needed this. I never realised how badly I needed this. I am going to forget about my home life. My past is my past. It is there for a reason. Tracy could never have been more right about tonight. I am lost in the music on the dance floor. I am dancing to the beat of my own drum. I am letting go of all the pain. I don't feel an ounce of panic or anxiety. Right now, I am invincible.

I am invincible to myself and everything I have been through.

Two hands grab my hips and keep me moving to the beat of the music. I can feel this person's warm breath on the back of my neck. "Keep moving Kate, if you stop now I will have to punish you" this person says into my ear. I keep moving, but internally I am frozen in place. To the outside, it would look like two people dancing to the music, but on the inside, I know this fucker works with the sick fucks I lived with.

I look for Tracy and see her eating some poor guys face. I really need to get her attention, but it's a bit hard when I can't move from this fuckwits hold. I have two options right now. Option one is to cause a scene. If I were to do that, no doubt I would be assaulted. Option two is to continue to dance and give in to this guy's demands.

I knew something was going to go wrong tonight. I knew letting my guard down was the wrong thing. But as Tracy always reminded me you only live once, so live it the right way. How wrong she was right now.

His hands keep travelling around my body, this is nothing new for me. I have been sexually assaulted since I was 16. I know how to desensitise myself to all the emotions. His lips attack my neck. Sucking and biting every chance he gets. I don't find this attractive. I know it is going to hurt when he gets his way with me.

Finally, I catch Tracy's attention. I try to tell her who this guy is with my eyes. She comes closer to me and grabs my hands. Pulling me to her, he loses his grip on my body. The look of shock on his face scares the crap out of me. I know he will do something and I will end up black and blue, or even worse, being buried six feet underground.

Tracy pushes me behind her. She is having a staredown with him. Now that I can see his face, I know who he is. He is one of my "fathers" lead henchmen. He always promised me he would find me until the day I die, whether at his hands or the universes. He moves towards Tracy and screams in her face. "Let the fucking whore go before a put a bullet through your head. But that will be after I make you watch me fuck her and slit her fucking throat".

Tracy never shows if she is scared. She stands up straighter. Even in her 5-inch heels, he towers over her, but she doesn't care. "You go anywhere near her, and I swear to fucking God, I will cut your fucking dick off and shove it so far up your arse you will cough up cum for the rest of your fucking life" she yells back at him.

His face scrunches up, and I can practically see the steam coming out of his ears. He looks directly at me and makes a gun with his finger and thumb. Doing the shooting action, he turns his back and walks away. Tracy keeps her back to me until we can't see him anymore. Once he was out of sight, she turns to me and pulls me into her. Holding me as tight as she possibly could. "Let's get out of here" she yells into my ear. I nod my head towards her, and she pulls me out of the club. We pass Sammy on the way out. He looks towards us both.

"I'll call you later" Tracy says to him. He nods his head, and she drags me out to the taxi rank. We are back at my apartment before I had even realised it. My brain is buzzing. I cannot concentrate on one thing. My adrenaline is making my heart rate pick up. I can feel the panic attack coming on, but there is no way to stop it. I don't usually panic when I am at my own place, but tonight something is off. My loungeroom is trashed. My couch has been torn apart.

The kitchen is just as bad. All my dishes are broken. Cutlery and utensils are all over the floor. Glass was broken in every nook and cranny. The rest of the apartment is much the same. My bedroom, well, what I think is my bedroom, has been torn apart. Written on the wall is the message that makes me drop to my knees.

"You can run, Kate, but you will never and I mean NEVER hide from me. I will track you down, find you and kill you as I should have five years ago".

Chapter 2- Running only causes problems.

B rad

I have been tasked to finding Kate and bringing her back to where she belongs. 4 years ago, she took off in the middle of the night. No one had seen Kate or heard from her in this time, but it is getting closer to her 21st birthday. We need to find her before then. Before the truth comes out over the news about her. John and Sally knew this was going to happen. If they had just done the right thing five years ago, we wouldn't be on a wild goose chase now.

Four years on the run is a very long time for any person. She should have shown her face around, but no one has seen her. The last known location for her was the hospital after she tried to kill herself. But once we made it to the hospital, she was gone. Discharged herself against her doctor's orders. She didn't give them an address of where she was going. We scrolled through the CCTV footage and saw she left with a blonde-haired little bitch.

We still haven't been able to find her either. How do two teenage girls just up and vanish during the night and from a hospital of all places?

Pacing the floor of my hotel room, Josh walks in. "New club tonight. We need to take a breather from finding the little slut" he says. I nod my head. "Why not?" I say back to him. We decide to hit up one of the hottest clubs the city has to offer. The line is around the corner. Luckily, Josh can pick locks as we are entering through the back of the club. Whoever saw us enter know not to ask questions.

We walk through the club like we own the joint. Girls are throwing themselves at us. We keep moving forwards, pushing the desperate whores out of our way. I stand at the bar, on the smaller side of the counter. The bartender holds up a beer towards me, and I give him a quick and short nod. I take notice of the people around me. I am scanning all their faces and checking them out to see if any of them are Kate.

I am not holding my breath, though. Kate has been elusive for a long time. I'm hoping to God she tried to kill herself again and succeeded this time around. Taking a quick chug of my beer, I keep looking around the club. A couple of girls approach the bar. I watch them but don't make it obvious. One of them leans over the bar and catches the bartender's attention. She orders a couple of drinks. The other girl is taking in her surroundings. I haven't seen her face, but I am hoping I get a look at it soon.

Two glasses of what looks to be red wine are placed in front of them. The first one picks hers up and starts drinking. The second girl takes a small sip and sets the glass back down. I nearly captured her face, but a silly dirty looking slut stood in my way. "Hey, baby" she calls out to me. I shake my head and tell her to scat with my hands. She doesn't get the point. "Come on hot stuff. How about you and I hit up the bathrooms for a quick fuck?" she asks. I move closer to her ear and yell into it.

"Back the fuck off slut or I will put a fucking bullet between your eyes" I tell her and flash her my gun. She takes a quick step back and moves away from me. "Just as I thought sweetheart" I say to myself. I grab my beer bottle back off the counter and take another quick swig. I look up towards the two girls at the counter. I finally get to see the second girl's face and can't believe my eyes.

There standing only feet away is the one and only elusive Katherine Fowley. The one girl who took off and tried to get away from us. I quickly pull my phone out and send off a message to John. I tell him I have found her and where she is located. He sends one back telling me to hurry the fuck up and get her to him. I give him a thumbs up and go back to watching her.

I follow her movements through the club. The friend she is with drags her to the dancefloor. I can tell she doesn't get out much as she looks like a deer caught in headlights right now. She watches the people around her and starts moving her body to the beat of the music. Her body hypnotises me. Forgetting why I am here in the first place.

"Fuck, is that her" Josh yells in my ear. I finally come out of my trance and nod my head yes at him. He goes to move towards her, and I grab hold of his arm. Shaking my head at him, letting him know I will be the one to get her. He stands down and allows me to do what I need to do before I approach her.

I wait until the timing is right. I need Kate to be in her own little world before I make my move. The song has changed multiple times before I make it to her. Her back is towards me, and I grab her hips. One wrong move on her part and I will take her body back in a body bag. I get close to her ear and tell her not to make any wrong moves. I can tell straight away that she knows who I am.

After four years, I finally have my hands on the girl who should have been dead. I keep us moving to the beat. I roam my hands around her body. I must admit I do miss her body. She would have been one of the best lays I have ever had. I don't care that she was only 16 and still a virgin when I took her. But fuck she was tight.

Exactly five years ago today, I took what I earnt. I'm hoping to fuck her again before I send her back to her daddy, for him to finish off the job finally. I kiss and nibble at her neck. I know this will turn her on. If it doesn't, I don't fucking care. I will get what I want. Maybe I'll shove my cock down her throat to get me all wet before I slam it in her tight hole. Just the thought of that tight little hole is making me hard.

Not paying any attention, Kate is pulled from my arms. I look at the little firecracker with her. I can tell I am going to have fun playing with this one too. I know Kate knows who I am now. I watch her face when she takes me in. I will have real pleasure watching the light leave her eyes when I take her back to John and Sally.

"Let the fucking whore go before a put a bullet through your head. But that will be after I make you watch me fuck her and slit her fucking throat" I tell the redhead in front of me. I don't know if she is stupid or drunk, but this little thing tries to stand up to my 6'5 frame. I could just fucking flick her in the head, and she would hit the ground. I watch as she stands up straighter. We are chest to chest now.

"You go anywhere near her, and I swear to fucking God, I will cut your fucking dick off and shove it so far up your arse you will cough up cum for the rest of your fucking life" she yells at me. I laugh at her threat but move away. I will give you girls this one. I know Kate is shitting herself right now. Before I leave, I make a shooting action towards Kate. Letting her know her days are numbered. I head towards the front of the club with Josh on my heels.

"What the fuck Brad? You fucking had her and just left her there?" Josh questions me. "Don't worry Josh. Once we take her and the little redhead bitch she is with, they will wish they never stood up to me. My phone starts ringing, and I answer it without looking at the caller. "What" I scream down the handset. "Is that any way to talk to your boss, boy?" John questions me. "What do I owe the pleasure of your phone call John?" I ask him. "Have you got that little whore with you?" he asks. As soon as I tell him I left her behind, he will rip shreds off my arse. "Nope. She's got a little firecracker on her side" I tell him honestly. "WHAT THE FUCK DO YOU MEAN YOU DON'T HAVE HER?" He screams down the phone. "Exactly what I said, John. If you had done what you fucking had to 5 years ago I wouldn't have to be running around the fucking countryside looking for her. I will give her tonight, but tomorrow she will be in hands and delivered to you" I tell him.

John hangs up on me. No sooner had I pocketed my phone, my message tone alerts me to new messages. I pull my phone out of my pocket and open the messages. They are pictures of what looks to be Kate's place. It has been trashed and slashed up. I know it was John. He would have been on his plane as soon as I had told him I found her.

Kate doesn't realise who she has for her parents. She ran from the wrong people, and now they are after her and won't stop until her body is limp and cold. It's a pity, though. She is a pretty young thing. She was born into the wrong family and was taken to her rightful owners as a baby. This year is when all the truth will come out. She doesn't need to know anything, though.

All will be revealed once she is back in John and Sally's care. Hopefully, we won't be waiting much longer.

Chapter 3- Broken homes go together with broken dreams.

K^{ate}

After Tracy and I got to mine and saw it trashed, she wanted to call the cops. I told her not to bother. They won't do anything, and when I did go to them when the abuse started, they did nothing to help me. I know exactly who broke in and trashed my place.

Trace takes me back to her place. She lives with a couple of roommates who don't like me. They think I am bad for Tracy. She is the life of the party, and I am a recluse. To stuck in my shell to be someone Tracy can rely on. I must agree with them, though. I am trouble. I have always been trouble, and I will be better off running again.

Tracy takes me straight into her bedroom. She throws a pair of trackies and a shirt at me and nods for me to put them on. I strip out of my clothes I was wearing and put on the clothes she gave me. I move towards the bed and pull the blankets back and climb in. "I'm so sorry, Tracy. I will find somewhere else in the morning to stay" I say to her. She turns to look at me, shock written all over her face. "Don't you ever apologise, you hear me. You will not be finding somewhere else to stay. Especially not when there are a bunch of fucktards after you."

Tracy climbs into the bed next to me. Pulling me into her arms and holding me tight. "I am never leaving your side, Kate. It would help if you believed me when I say this. I have no idea what those people are capable of, but I will protect you with my life" she tells me. I wish I could tell her everything that I know. I don't want her to become collateral damage because of me. We both snuggle down into the bed. Tracy falls asleep quickly, which leaves me staring at the walls and ceiling. I know sleep won't come to me tonight.

Morning comes quicker than I would like it to. I did not get even one second of sleep. My mind just kept replaying what Brad had said to me. Nothing in this world is now making any sense to me. They want me dead. Why? What have I done to deserve this? What God did I kill in a past life? But of course, none of the answers will come to me. Not when my brain is also asking why the grass is green? And why is the sky blue? Why is my life such a clusterfuck?

When Tracy starts stirring, I pretend I am asleep. She has work today, so once she has left, I will make my move. I need to get away from her. I need to keep her safe and away from my life's fuck ups. I lay in her bed, pretending I am asleep for what feels like hours. Tracy kisses my head and whispers that she'll be back later. 'I won't be' I think to myself. I know she will be so mad when she gets home from work, but her life and the lives of her friends and family need to be saved from my downfall.

I hear the click-clack of heels on the floor outside the bedroom door. I concentrate on listening to the footsteps until they are out of the front door. Tracy's roommates are still in the apartment. I'm pretty confident they won't say anything when I leave. They usually glare at me until I feel so uncomfortable that I will leave anyway.

I wait another 10 minutes before I climb out of bed. I take off Tracy's clothes and leave them folded neatly on the bed. I redress in what I wore last night and make my move. I quickly use the bathroom, then leave the house. Her roommates didn't say a word.

Getting out to the main road, I have a decision to make. What way do I go? Going left would take me back to my apartment. Going right will take me to the city limits, and then I would be lost in the big wide world. On the spur of the moment, I go right. Heading back towards my apartment would be a big mistake. They would have eyes on the place, and the minute I walk in, they would swoop in and who knows what would happen to me.

I walk the road, nowhere in mind. I have no idea where I am going. I left all my personal belongings at Tracy's. There is no way she can track me now. The wind is harsh against my skin, the sun's rays are blinding me, but I keep moving. I cannot stop now. I need to get away from everything I ever knew and hope to God I make it through all of this.

I wish I knew where I belonged. John and Sally, my 'parents', were fantastic when I was a child. The moment I turned 13, I became their slave. I would have to cook and clean for them. I would also have to clean John. He would make me go into the bathroom with him and wash him. The sexual abuse started when I was 15. I would try and fight them, to stop touching me, but my screams and cries would go unheard. I thought Sally would have wanted to save me, but she would turn a blind eye.

I've walked, and I've walked some more. I have no idea where I am now. I have no idea where I am going. All I know is that I am lost, and the sun is beginning to set. My stomach is grumbling, and my legs are sore. My body is wanting to rest, but my brain is telling me to keep moving. If I stop now, they will find me.

All that surrounds me now are bushes and trees. I need to sit for a minute. My legs are like jelly. I collapse onto the soft grass and lean my back against the tree trunk that is behind me. My eyes close on their own. I am startled awake by someone shaking my shoulder.

"AHHHHHHHHHHHHHHHHHHHHHHHHHHHH" I scream. The person takes a step back. "Shit sorry. I was making sure you were still alive" he says to me. I look at his face, he isn't someone I recognise.

"I'll go. I'm sorry if this is your property" I tell him. He gives me a small smile, and I try to stand up. My legs are weak, I use the tree trunk to help me to my feet, I go to take one step, and I fall forward. This man quickly grabs me. "You won't be going anywhere. My house is just over that hill, let me help you there, get you some food and water" he says. I shake my head no and try to push myself off him.

"Don't fight me, please. My wife will look after you, I promise" he says. I eventually give in. I know I need some food to be able to keep moving. He picks me up and carries me over the hill. His house is more like a prison compound. My heart starts racing in my chest. I am going from one prison to another. He can tell I am stressing. "Don't. I promise you will not be hurt here" he says, trying to calm my racing heart.

As we get closer, I can see what looks like hundreds of motorcycles, all lined up in a row. Men of all shapes and sizes, walking around the lot. As soon as we made it into the compound, all eyes were on us. I shrunk back into this man's chest. My body was shaking like a leaf. "Step back boys" he yells out. I cover my ears to stop the noise. My brain is running a million miles an hour, with thoughts that I should not be having.

He walks us up the steps to the main property, and the door is opened by another man wearing a leather vest. I don't take much notice of what is written on the vest. The inside is loud, and I keep my hands on my ears to block out the noise as much as possible. The place smells like stale beer and tobacco. It reminds me of John's breath, every time he would come into my room of a night.

The woman in the room, rushed like mad when the man brought me in. Questions on what happened? Where was I found? Who was I, and why was I on their property? All the questions were coming in at once until the man holding me shouted. "ALL OF YOU BACK THE FUCK OFF NOW" he yelled at the women. They all retreated to where they came from. One more woman came forward.

She was dressed in the same leather vest the men were. "What have you found, babe?" she asked the man holding me. "Found her up against a tree just on the outskirts of the land. Food, water, and a warm bed is all she needs" he says to her. She nods her head and follows us as the man took off again, up a couple of flights of stairs and down a corridor. "She'll stay on our floor. Away from all the fucktards down there" he says to her. "I fully agree" she answers back.

She opens the door to a room, and he takes me in and places me on the bed. I try to sit up straight away, but my arms give out on me. "Just rest sweetie. I will bring you some fresh clothes and food after you have a rest" the woman says to me. She sits next to me on the bed and rubs my forehead. "Rest Princess. Close your eyes. You are safe here" she says as my eyes close on their own.

I wake when I hear voices coming from the outside of the room I am in. I strain my ears to listen to what they are saying. "Do you think it's her?" a male's voice comes through. "I don't know, but the only way to find out is to ask her when she wakes up" comes a female's voice. I sit up in the bed and swing my legs over the side. Taking a couple of deep breaths, I stand up, wobbling as I do so. I find my shoes on the floor next to the bed. I quickly slip my feet into them and tiptoe over to the door.

The talking had stopped by then. I quietly opened the door and stuck my head out. Looking both ways, I notice the coast was clear. Stepping out of the room, I didn't know which way to go. I slowly started walking down the hallway, it came to a dead end. Cursing softly to myself, I turned around, a scream leaving my lips. "Shit sorry, I didn't mean to scare you" comes the rough gravelly voice of a man.

I fall to the floor and hug my knees to my chest. The panic is running rampant through my veins. "Oh, shit" the man exclaims. He kneels on the floor next to me, rubbing my back and applying pressure between my shoulder blades. My breathing is in short sharp pants. Nothing he was doing was working. He grabs my hand and places it on his chest. "Follow my breathing. In, out. In, out" he commands.

I follow his breathing and start to calm mine down. "That's it, sweetheart. In and out. You are doing a fantastic job" he complimented me. "What the fuck is going on here?" another gruff voice calls out. "Sorry, Pres. Found her in the hall. She turned around, and just the sight of me sent her into a panic" this guy says to the other guy known as his Pres.

The Pres guy nods his head and looks towards me. "You alright now, princess?" he asks me. I shake my head once and start to lift myself off the floor. The other guy holds his hand out to help me. "I won't bite, I promise. I'm just going to make sure when you stand you don't fall again" he tells me. I take his hand, and he helps pull me to my feet. "Thank you," I say to him. He hums a little in acknowledgement at my thanks.

The men lead me down the stairs into the main hall. All around the room are leather-clad women and more tough and scary looking biker men. I can feel my heart rate picking up again. The Pres walks in front of me, and the other guy is behind us. He must have noticed my back going stiff as we walked into the room. He gently placed his hand on my shoulder, "no one will hurt you here. We all just look scary. Most of those men are giant teddy bears" he whispers to settle my nerves.

We walk into the kitchen. The lady who helped us out was in there cooking something at the stove. "What would you like to eat sweetie?" she asks me. I shrug my shoulders, "Just a piece of bread if you have any?" I say back to her. The men both laugh at my answer. "Oh, sweetheart, you can eat more than that here. If you want pancakes with chocolate sauce and fruit, you've got it" the Pres man says to me.

"Can I ask a question?" I ask them all in the room. All 3 nod their heads towards me. "Who are you, and where am I?" I ask. The one known as Pres steps forward. "That was two questions there princess," he says with a laugh. "Sorry" I whisper. "Don't be sorry. I'm Bones, this here is Buster" he points to his left, "And this wonderful woman is my 'Old lady'" he points to his right, wrapping his arm around her. "I'm Casey," she says.

"This is the 'Devils on Wheels' MC" as soon as those words were out of Bones' mouth, I feel my heart rate pick up. I have heard about these guys. They are ruthless when it comes to violence. I know John feared them, he would always say that he would love to watch them burn to the ground.

Casey notices my breathing change after Bones had said who they were. She came and stood next to me. "We won't hurt you, princess, but you need to tell us who you are and who you are running from" she whispers into my ear. "We will protect you" Buster chimes in. I close my eyes, willing my breathing to slow down.

"My name is Katherine Fowley," I tell them. All three of them turn to look at each other. "It is her" Casey whispers more to herself, but we all hear her. "Butch is going to be so fucking happy when he hears she is here," she says a bit louder. I couldn't help myself. I needed to know who this 'Butch' person is. "Who is Butch?"

All three look at me and reply at the same time.

"Your father."

Chapter 4- The truth begins

Kate

I have no clue what happened. One minute I was sitting at the table and talking to Bones, Buster, and Casey then the next thing I know, I am laying on the floor. My head is pounding, I don't know whether it is from a headache or what, but all I know is that it's sore. Bones is kneeling beside me. "Katherine, can you hear me?" he asks.

I let out a soft sigh and raise my hands to my head. I try to release the pressure and the pain, but nothing seems to be working. "Get Meds in here now" I hear one of them say. I have my eyes closed, so I don't know who spoke. More footsteps can be heard in the room now. "What happened?" is the only question flying from people's mouths.

"Everyone get out" I can hear a female's voice say. It sounded like Casey. "Tracker, can you get in contact with Butch?" I hear Casey ask someone. I don't hear any noise from the person named 'Tracker', and with my eyes still closed, I can't see if he or she nodded their head. I try to open my eyes, but it is like they are glued shut.

"Buster, help me get her off the floor," Bones says. Both men pick me up from the floor and lay me down on what must be the table. "Katherine, I need you to open your eyes, Princess. I need to make sure you are ok?" Bones says in my ear. I can feel my eyes flutter, but I still cannot get them to open fully. I can feel the softness of someone's hand rubbing my head. "Come on, Princess. Get those eyes opened for us" comes the soft voice of Casey.

I force my eyes to flutter again, slowly opening them, blinking them shut as soon as the light hits them. I blink a few more times. I am adjusting to the bright light hanging above my head. "Oh, Jesus fuck, my head hurts" I cry out. Casey softly giggles. "That's a new one," she says. "Jesus fuck, alright," Bones says with a laugh. Another voice cuts through the room, "What have we got here?" he asks. "Meds meet Katherine. Princess here fainted and hit her head on the table when she went down" Bones tells who I am now assuming to be Meds.

"Hi, Katherine. I'm Meds. I'm the club's doctor. Can you tell me where it hurts?" he asks me. "My head" is all I can say. He flashes a light into my eyes and feels around my head. I have no idea what he is looking for. "Get her into a room. She has a concussion, and someone will need to stay with her for the next few hours, waking her every 2 hours. Otherwise, she should be fine" Meds says to the room.

Buster picks me up and carries me bridal style, "What room was she in?" he asks. "2 doors down from us" I hear Casey respond. Buster grunts and carries me out of the kitchen, back out to the main room, and towards the stairs. Everyone in the room all stopped what they were doing and watched as Buster carried me up the stairs. "Do you think it's true? She really is Butch's little girl?" I hear one woman ask another. "Not sure but we will find out soon enough" another one answers.

Buster gets me into the room and lays me on the bed. "Sleep Princess. I will wake you in 2 hours" he says to me while tucking me in. I don't argue, and I allow my eyes to close into a dreamless sleep.

True to his word, 2 hours later, Buster is waking me up. "Fuck off and let me fucking sleep" I yell at him. He laughs a deep rumbling belly laugh. "You really are Butch's daughter," he says. "Go back to sleep, Princess," he tells me. I roll over and get comfortable once again. Not before long, I am woken by a commotion from down the stairs.

"Where the fuck is she" I hear someone yell out. Buster stands and guards the door, not knowing who is here. "Butch calm the fuck down" more voices are yelling out. I sit up in the bed when I hear the name, Butch. Tears fall from my eyes. In my 21 years of life, I have never been so fucking happy and sad to know that my birth father is here to rescue me.

I swing my legs over the side of the bed and try to stand up. I sway a little when I finally get onto my feet. Buster walks over to me. "Where do you think you're going, Princess?" he asks me. "To see my father," I tell him. Buster wraps his arm around my waist, "Let me help you?" he asks me. I wrap my arm around his neck and let him lead me out of the room and down the stairs.

Once at the bottom, the room is going wild. This Butch guy has all these tough-looking bikers on high alert. "Where is Butch?" Buster asks. "Chapel" is the response he gets. He helps me over to 2 huge doors. Buster knocks on the door, and we wait for someone to call out 'come in'. Once we get that, he opens the door slowly.

This room is enormous. The table in the middle of the room is the length of my apartment. It has at least forty to fifty chairs around it. I look to the right, and there is no one sitting there. I move my head to the left and at the end of the table are four people. Two of them are Bones and Casey. The other two, I don't know who they are, but they both look scary as fuck.

"Butch, Diana" Buster calls. Butch and Diana turn around to look at us. I gasp once I see the woman. It is like I am looking in a mirror. My heart rate increases and my breathing is coming out in short little puffs. Buster quickly moves me to a chair and sits me down. He rubs in between my shoulder blades again. "Just breath with me, Princess. It will pass over soon" he says to me. He places my hand on his chest again. "Breathe with me. In and out. In and out" he says

I look up again at the two other people in the room. The woman is crying. Tears are falling fast from her eyes. The man has his arm wrapped around her. He also has tears falling down his cheeks. "Holy fucking dog shit. It really is her" the woman, Diana, calls out. I can tell she wants to come over to me. Once I know my breathing is calm, I slowly stand up, using Buster as a leaning pole.

As soon as I am up on my feet and steady, I move quickly over to Butch and Diana. Butch wraps his arm around me and pulls me into his chest. His other arm is wrapped around Diana and pulls her into his other side. She wraps one of her arms around me and the other around Butch. We all stand here for what feels like forever—holding onto each other for dear life.

I try to remember if John or Sally ever held me like this, but I cannot think of a time where they showed me any kind of love and care. "We'll give you guys some space," Bones says. He, Casey, and Buster leave the room, the doors closing quietly behind them. I can hear all the people cheer once Bones, Casey, and Buster get out there. Butch steps back from us, and Diana quickly wraps me up in both of her arms.

"I can't believe you are really here," Butch says. "After 21 fucking years, we finally have you back in our arms" he continues. All I want to do is break down and tell them everything that has happened to me over the past 21 years, but I know as soon as I open my mouth Butch will destroy everything in his way. Diana leads us to a couple of chairs, and we sit down. She takes my face in her hands.

"You look exactly like me. It's uncanny" Diana says. I look at them both. "How did you guys get here so quickly? When I found out I was kidnapped, I was told I was flown halfway around the world" I ask them. Both Butch and Diana look at each other with confusion written on their faces. "Katherine, we live four towns over from here. As soon as Tracker said they might have found you, I floored it here. Where did you grow up?" Butch asks me. "Old Town," I tell him. "FUCK" Butch screams out. "You were only a two day drive away from us. Why the fuck did it take us 21 fucking years to find you?" he questions himself.

The truth is finally coming out. No wonder John and Sally feared the Devil's on Wheels. They stole me from one of the members. "Who raised you?" Diana asks me quietly. I can tell she was nervous to ask that question. "John and Sally Fowley. Well, I think they are their names. I am not sure anymore" I tell her. I can see Butch from the corner of my eye. He has steam coming out of his ears, and his face is bright red.

"Dad?" I call out. He looks at me, and I can see him calm himself down. "Yeah, Princess?" he asks. "Do you know them?" I ask him. I am nervous about his response. "Unfortunately, the people you called mum and dad for the past 21 years are your aunt and uncle," he tells me. I can tell he is getting angry by the change of his voice in the middle of his reply.

So, my Aunt and Uncle stole me as a baby. One of them is blood-related to either one of my parents. This is all so confusing, and again my head is hurting. I place my head in my hands and massage my temples, hoping that will relieve the pressure. "What is wrong, Princess?" my mum asks me. "I have a headache," I tell her honestly.

A knock is sounded at the door. Butch walks over and opens it. Standing in the doorway is Meds. "Sorry, Butch. But I need to check on Katherine. She fainted earlier and hit her head on the table in the kitchen" Meds tells my dad. He grunts and lets him in. Meds takes one look at me and shakes his head. "Why didn't you tell anyone you were in pain?" he asks me. I shrug my shoulders not having an answer for him right now.

He does his checks and hands me two pills and a bottle of water. "Just normal over the counter pain pills. Can't give you anything stronger. Take these and get some more rest" he tells me. Butch comes over to me and picks me up bridal style. "What room have you been staying in?" he asks me. "I'm not sure. You will have to ask Casey" I tell him. He carries me out of the chapel room into the main room again.

Everyone stops what they are doing and turn to face us. Casey approaches us. "What room?" is all Butch asks. "Third floor, 2nd door on the right," she tells him. "Thanks," he says quietly and heads towards the stairs. Butch takes the stairs slowly, so my head isn't bouncing. Following behind us is Diana. She is still crying. I don't know if it's because they have found me or because of who took me.

Making it into the room, Butch lays me down gently. Diana tucks me in and climbs onto the bed next to me. "I'll stay with her," she tells Butch. He nods his head and leans down to kiss my forehead. "I'll be downstairs," he tells us. "Get some rest, Princess. We have a lot of catching up to do" he tells me, turns, and walks out of the room.

Diana wraps me up in her arms, kisses my forehead, and holds me tight to her. My eyes get heavy, and I try to fight the inevitable, but sleep wins. I fall asleep, wrapped in the warmth and love, I have craved ever since I was a child.

Chapter 5- When the bullets start flying.

B rad

"Where the fuck did that little whore go?" I have asked myself that question at least a hundred times in the past 20 minutes. I have John breathing down my neck every 3.7 seconds, wondering if I have found her. He knows if she makes it over the city limits and into DOW's territory, his sick game will be found out. I am also worried about that cause that means I have lost my plaything.

She ran, and she ran good. Once she noticed her apartment was trashed, she took off with her friend. That is who I need to find. She will know where she is. I will make sure the friend talks before I slit her little throat. She is a good for nothing little tramp who needs to learn her fucking place in this world. She back chats the wrong person, and she will end up with a bullet between her eyes.

I make it my mission to find the little red-headed bitch. She is my ticket to finding that whore of a thing who thought running would be easy. She got away four years ago. Never again, under my watch.

I scoured the streets for her. I need to find out where she lives. Rough her up until she talks. "Fucking hell. Where the fuck does the bitch live?" I ask myself. I follow the steps I have taken repeatedly. I come to Kate's apartment again. There is movement inside the apartment. I rush in and up the stairs. Hopefully, Kate has come back, and this will be an easy swoop in, capture, and return to where her final resting place will be.

I open the door to her apartment and quietly walk in. Nothing seems to have been moved from when I was last in here. I hear a noise coming from the bedroom. I make my way towards the hallway when the sound of gunfire hits my ears. I quickly pull my gun out of the holster, taking off the safety. I move to stand behind the wall, the only protection I have right now.

Footsteps can be heard coming out of the bedroom. I slowly raise my gun, look around the corner and nearly fall on my arse when I feel the cold metal of a gun being pressed against my skull. "Hello, Bradley. It has been a long time since I've seen you nephew" comes the deep gravelly voice of the one and only Butch.

"Uncle Butch. So good to see you again. Where is that little whore of yours? She needs to pay for her crimes she has committed against my stepfather" I tell him, with a smirk on my face. "Oh Bradley, the only crime that has been committed is you and your family still breathing. Today I will let you live, but mark my words boy and make sure you run home and tell the rest of them. I am coming for you all, and when I get you, you will all be tied up by your ankles and slit open from your hips to your chin" Butch says in my ear.

I am roughly shoved forward and hit the ground on my knees. The footsteps retreat out of the apartment, but words are being yelled at me again. "Remember to tell your worthless family what the plan is boy. Judgement day will be upon you all very, very soon" are the last words I hear from the bunch of fucktards as they leave.

I know now that once I get back and tell John and Sally, war will be upon us. I don't know whether I am excited about this or shitting bricks over it. I know those arseholes are ruthless when it comes to fighting, but I also know that we are just as bad. The only problem we have is the fact that they have more numbers. John better be prepared for this shit.

Making it back to John's makeshift home, slamming doors behind me, John rushes out to see what the commotion is all about. "What has gotten into you, boy? And where the fuck is Katherine?" he yells out. "Bad news John. She's back with Butch" I tell him. All the colour drains from John's face. I can see the sweat start to form and roll down his cheeks. The slight shake to his body lets me know he knows shit is about to go down.

"The message from your brother is to be prepared. War is on us, and we are fucked" I tell him.

John shakes his head. "No, we are going to get the bitch and fucking kill her. He is the reason I don't have my beautiful Jane with me. That is why I am stuck with your whore of a mother. An eye for a fucking eye, Bradley. Don't you forget it" John yells out.

I know his words should anger me about my mother, but they don't. She is a whore. She sleeps with whoever she wants. At one point she even tried to leave to get with one of those MC scum bags. John should have killed her then, but he didn't. "FUCK" John screams out again. He knows this is all about to end in bloodshed. He just hopes it's not his.

"We need to find her and get her away from them. This is fucked. Sick and tired of him getting everything handed to him, and I get the leftovers. Butch needs to learn a fucking lesson. I couldn't get Diana so I will go for the next best thing. Katherine will be back with me by the end of this week. She would be at one of their clubhouses. Search all of them" John yells out.

Josh and I start planning out our attacks. I need to make sure we hit the right one first. "She would be in the closest one to us. She wouldn't have gotten far by foot" Josh says as he starts pulling up maps on his computer. "That is true, but who is to say she hasn't been moved to another site since then," I say to him. We both look hard at all the Devil's areas around.

They have the majority of land around the tri-state area. Knowing we have a lot of ground to cover means we must get our arses into gear now. Making plans to find Katherine is going to be hard. Being caught is instant death for us. We must move like ninjas, but knowing Josh, he will get us noticed. Maybe I can do this on my own.

I wait for nightfall to start my mission. I don't let on to anyone where I am going. I just move. Silently, I go towards the closest clubhouse. I know she will either be here or at her father's. I need to find her, and I need to find her quickly. I don't care what it is going to cost me in the end. I need to help John get rid of her. She knows too much, and that is not good for us.

Getting into the compound was easy. Bikers are all drunk and stoned by now, so getting through into the house won't be difficult either. All I need is a leather vest, and I'll be in. I see a lone prospect standing at the gate, keeping watch on the main road. Target one will be down in seconds. I make my approach keeping my feet light. I apply my silencer to my gun, and as soon as I am close enough, I raise my weapon and shoot.

Hitting my target where I intended, a clean shot through the back of his head. I walk over to his body and remove the prospect vest from his back. Knowing now I have an in, I just have to keep my head down and move quickly. Putting the vest on my own back, I make my way towards the main doors. Slowly opening the door to assess my situation. The room is dark like everyone has gone to bed.

"Jackpot" I whisper to myself. I move quickly, keeping my noise levels down. I make it to the stairs. Taking two at a time, I make it to the third level. It is eerily quiet walking down the hallway, but I keep going. She has to be here. I open every door I come across, and all of them are empty. Not one soul is in this place. All their bikes are out the front.

I head up to the fourth floor, not a soul on the third. I open every door I come across and again, nothing, nada, zip. This floor is empty like the others. "Fuck" I whisper to myself. I head back down to the main floor. This building is vacant, which confuses me more. "Bikes out front, but no one here. What the fuck is going on?" I ask myself as I step off the last step onto the main floor.

Still, no noise and no lights are on. I walk towards the main doors and open them, stepping outside. Going down a couple of steps, I'm ambushed. I am back on my knees, with a gun against my head. "What ya doing here, boy?" the voice of Butch comes through. "Fuck off dickhead. I am here to take the little slut you call a daughter. Need to stick my dick in her tight hole once more, before she dies a slow and painful death" I tell him, with a smirk on my face.

Next thing I know, I am lying face down on the gravel. "You fucking hit me you arsewipe" I yell out to Butch. "Next time you won't be talking back to me," he says to me, with his own little smirk. "You'll never find her, though. She is in hiding, far away from here" Butch continues.

"I'm fucked" is all I can think to myself. "Get this piece of shit out of my face" Butch screams at the boys around me. Two of the guys grab me from under my arms. "Bradley, thank your lucky fucking stars that I didn't end you tonight. You will come in handy finding my brother" Butch all but yells in my face. The guys who have me in their arms, drag me towards the gate where I shot the prospect. His body is no longer there, but the gates open and I am thrown out onto the rock gravel in front of the gate.

I can feel the blood already rolling down my face from where I have hit the gravel. "Stay off my property, or next time I will put a few hundred bullets through your body and leave you hanging out the front of your mother's house," one of the guys says to me. I don't make a noise, I get up, brush myself off and head off in the direction of where I parked my car. Knowing full well, if I am caught again, I will be a dead man.

Chapter 6- Hiding in plain sight.

- -

K ate

Laying on the bed in a hotel room, Mum is pacing the floor. "Please, mum, can you take a break. The carpet has your foot tracks, and they will probably charge us more for the damage" I say to her. She turns her head to look at me and just smiles. Tears are filling her eyes again. "I just can't believe you are here with me, after so long. I thought you were dead. I am just nervous that they will take you again" she says to me.

Diana, I mean mum, had sat me down when we got here and told me the complete truth on what had happened in the past and the reason why I was taken from her and Butch. "Mum?" I call her name. "Yeah, Kate?" "Did John take me because of Jane's death?" I ask her again. I know the answer, but I just want to make sure I have all the facts correct.

"At the time, John blamed us for her death. We didn't get her killed, and we didn't kill her. The person responsible left one of our prospect cuts. Three days later, our prospect was found hanging from his ankles, gutted, which is our signature. It was either a lone rider or a copycat who did it" Mum explains to me.

"So, they took me for revenge?" I ask her. She sadly nods her head in answer. "Did you know that they were meant to kill me by my 16th birthday?" I ask her. She looks at me with confusion. "They were going to kill you?" she asks me. I nod my head. "I got out of there four years ago, and when I tried to commit suicide. My best friend saved my life. She was a complete stranger going on a walk and came across me, tying a noose to a tree. She stopped me and saved me that day" I tell mum.

I watched as the tears fell from her eyes. "They wanted to kill you?" she says more to herself than to me. It was like the words I had just told her were finally sinking in. Diana screams as loud as she can and throws a lamp from the bedside table to the wall on the opposite side of the room. I quickly stand and grab hold of her. "They failed. I am still here. Please, I know this is difficult, but I need you to stay level headed" I tell her while holding her in my arms.

Diana pulls away from me and wipes her eyes. "I need to make a phone call. I'll be just outside this door. Do not, and I mean it, Kate, do not open the door. If I know John and Sally, they will already have people out there looking for you" Diana says. I nod my head and go and sit in the corner of the room, away from the door. Diana leaves the room and slams the door behind her. I get up out of the corner and curl myself up in a ball on the couch. Closing my eyes, wishing this nightmare would be over.

I don't know how long I was asleep for, but loud voices wake me. Scared that John has found me, I rush into the bathroom and close the door, locking it behind me. I climb into the bathtub, hoping that this hiding spot will keep me safe, but also knowing that if it is John, I'm fucked. The yelling stops, and instead, I hear footsteps moving around in the room.

"Kate, are you in there?" the male's voice calls while knocking on the door. I don't make a sound, in case it is John or even Brad.

"Katie, it's Butch. Shit. Kate, it's ok to come out. I promise you it's Butch" he calls through the door. A softer feminine voice comes through. "Kate, honey. It's Diana. I promise. They are not here. It's just us. Come out please" she pleads with me. I slowly pull myself out of the tub and walk over to the door. Unlocking it slowly not to make too much noise, I open it just enough for me to look out and see that it is just Butch and Diana.

Opening the door fully, Butch pulls on my free arm, straight into his chest. He holds me tightly to him. "I'm never letting you out of my sight again, Kate. I promise. You are safe with us" he whispers into my hair. I feel my body relax at his words. I feel safe in his arms. "Come on, Princess, let's get some food and hit the road. We have a bit of a drive ahead of us" Butch says.

Sitting in the back seat of the truck, the door opens on the other side, and another person climbs in. He has his back to me before he climbs in. I feel my heart rate accelerate and my breathing coming out in short sharp bursts. "Oh, shit, Princess. It's only me. Buster. I'm sorry I should have announced myself" he says as he climbs in next to me. "Just breathe Kate. Here, feel my breathing" he says as he grabs my hand and places it on his chest.

Once my breathing has finally settled, and my heart rate slowly comes back down, I look out the window to see Butch and Diana watching us. Butch was scowling, but Diana had a smile on her face. I can see Butch's lips moving but can't hear what he is saying. Diana then slaps him in the chest and says something back to him. The smile is off her face now. I rest my head on the window of the door and close my eyes. My body is exhausted, as is my mind and soul. Sleep comes easily to me.

The next time I open my eyes, the car is slowly pulling up into another compound looking place. Buster grabs my hand, and I look at him. "This is where Butch and Diana live. Everyone here will look after you" he whispers to me. I look at him and then move my eyes to the outside. People. People are everywhere. Bikes are revving, and my heart rate increases with every rev of the throttle.

Buster holds my hand and helps me out of the truck. Butch and Diana watch him. Butch has a scowl on his face still, and Diana has a soft, warm smile. "Welcome home, Princess," Diana says to me. I look around at all the new faces in the compound. Butch stands up on the top step of the clubhouse porch and calls for everyone's attention.

"Ladies and Gentlemen, this fine young lady standing with Diana today is my daughter Katherine. She is to be treated with the utmost respect. If I catch any of you treating her like dirt, you will meet the bottom of my boots, as they stomp on your fucking faces. Do I make myself clear?" Butch yells out. The chorus of "Yes Pres" that rings out from the rest of the men and woman was unanimous.

Butch comes down and puts his arm around my shoulders, "We need to chat little lady" he says to me. I nod my head and follow him into the clubhouse. Buster leaves me at the door. I look back at him, and he nods his head towards Butch and mouths "you'll be fine Princess" to me. I turn back towards Butch and continue following him in the clubhouse into what looks like an office.

Butch holds the door open, and I take a seat in front of his desk. He closes the door and places his hand in mine. "Sit on the couches. They are more comfortable and less formal" he says. I follow him to the couch and sit down in the middle seat. Butch sits to my left, and Diana is to my right. "Just before we left town, we had a little run-in with Bradley. He mentioned something about having you again. It would be best if you told me everything, Katherine. I want all the information" he says. "Please" he adds on.

I take a deep breath and look to the floor. "What do you want to know?" I ask him. "Everything, Katherine. I want to know everything" he says to me. I can feel the first of many tears fall down my face. "As soon as I turned 16, John and Bradley raped me. They raped me every night after that" I tell them. The gasp from Diana's mouth makes my tears fall even faster.

"I'm going to fucking kill the lot of them. String them up by their fucking ankles and watch the life drain out of them" Butch yells. He jumps up from the couch and punches a hole into the wall. I jump at his outburst, and Diana quickly wraps her arms around me. "Shhhh, baby. It'll be ok" she whispers into my hair.

I know her words are meant to be comforting, but right now in this very moment. I feel like my world is falling apart. I don't know where I belong. All I know is that I am about to be in the biggest fight of my life. I say a little prayer to whoever will listen to me, that I come out of this alive and in one piece. I know what John is capable of. I just hope Butch is ready for this fight.

A knock at the door brings me out of my own little world. Butch answers the door. "What?" he yells out to the person on the other side. "We have visitors, and I don't think you are going to be very happy," the voice on the other side of the door says. "Stay here. Do not come out until I say you can" Butch says to me. He nods his head at Diana, and she stands up. "It'll be ok, baby. I will be back soon" she says to me.

They leave the room and lock the door behind them. I hate not knowing what is going on. I try to open the lock, but it is stuck. "Great, back to being locked up in fucking rooms. They are very much like each other" I say to myself about Butch and John. I lay down on the couch and close my eyes. I have nothing else to do while I am in this room, so I may as well sleep.

I had no sleep. As soon as I laid down and closed my eyes, shouting voices could be heard. I knew straight away who was here. John. He has found me. FUCK. I move the couch off the wall and climb down behind it. I need to hide. This isn't the best hiding place, but it is all I can manage for now. Pulling the couch back as far as I could get it, I wait. I wait until there is no more yelling. I wait for any other noises to stop.

Once I think the coast is clear, a gunshot can be heard, ringing through the building. My heart rate skyrockets, my breathing becomes erratic. I hear more screaming, but the sounds are muffled. I can't even hear my own thoughts properly. My vision becomes blurred, with black spots dancing all around. I let the darkness consume me until there is nothing there.

Chapter 7

B^{utch}

My Princess has been through the fucking ringer. All I know now is that I want to kill all of them. John, Sally, Bradley, and anyone else who has anything to do with him. They stole my baby and then stole her innocence. I am scared that they have stolen a lot more from her. Katherine, she is timid as a mouse and now finding out what they did to her......

I can't finish my thought as I make my way down into the common room. Upon entering, I notice the piece of shit who will die by my hands. Blood or not. He crossed a fucking line and will pay for it all.

"Where is my little whore?" he opens his mouth. My VP pulls out his gun and points it in John's direction. "Standing next to you, it seems" my VP Raider responds. Raider places his hand on my shoulder and nods his head at me. He is telling me quietly that he will handle this bullshit.

"Who the fuck are you to talk about my wife like that?" John snarls out. Without missing a beat, "Who the fuck are you to come in here and call your wife a whore?" Raider says. My boys all chuckled at that. Raider stands there with a smirk plastered on his face. "I should put a fucking bullet in your head, you piece of..." "Don't finish that sentence sweetheart" Diana pipes up and shuts Sally down.

"How about you all get your filthy arses off my property. You do that now, and you all leave with your lives. I'll even count to ten. Giving you a three-second head start" I tell them. John steps towards me. "An eye for an eye brother. Don't forget that. I will have your little whore of a daughter, and she will be strung up like my Jane was because of you fucks" he spits in my face.

I see red. My right fist swings out and connects with John's face. He stumbles back and hits the floor. Bradley steps forward to help John but is restrained by Buster. "If I were you, little boy, I would stop moving" Buster yells in his ear. John pulls himself back up from the floor, blood dripping from his lip. "This isn't the end, Baxter. I will have her, and when I get her, I will fucking kill her" He spits out at me.

I go to swing my fist again, but Diana stops me. Instead, she steps forward and punches him, square in the nose. You could hear the bones break from every corner in the room. "You touch my daughter again, I will be the one who strings you up, cut your dick off and shove it so far down your fucking throat, you will choke to death on it" she spits in his face.

One of his goons pulls his gun out, pointing it at Diana. The boy must be stupid if he thinks he will be quick enough in a room full of bikers. "Drop the fucking gun" Savage calls out. This cock stain releases the safety and cocks the pistol, still pointing it at Diana. "Pull the fucking trigger" Sally screams out to him. Savage whips his own gun out and pulls his trigger. Blowing the brains of this cock wank all over the clubhouse wall.

"One down. How many more of you wankers want to play?" Savage asks the room. All of John's boys step back and lower weapons. "Are you for real? Put them back up and kill all the fuckers in this room" Sally cries out. Diana steps up to her, "You wanna play chicken with your life, Sally?" she asks her. Sally's face pales, and she takes a step back. "Just as I thought. All bark and no bite" Diana says to her and steps back to stand next to me.

"If I were you, I would leave and never show your faces again. If one hair on my daughter's head is out of place because of you, I will finish you" I tell them. All of John's boys and himself leave through the door. We wait until they have left the property before we relax. "Someone clean this fucking mess up. I have a daughter to get back to" I say to the room.

The prospects get into gear and start cleaning up the body and blood. They already know where to put the body. I grab Diana's hand and pull her back to my office. Unlocking the door and opening it slowly, we don't see Katherine anywhere. "Kate" no response. "Katie" I call again to no response. "KATHERINE" I yell her name. Diana has entered the room and is looking in any spot she can think of. She moves the couch.

"I have her. FUCK" she cries out. In two steps, I am looking at what Diana is looking at. There curled up in a little ball is Katherine. I pick her up and lay her on the couch. "Fuck. Get Doc in here" I tell Diana. She quickly runs out of the room, screaming for Doc. I sit on my knees next to Katherine and rub her head. "Come on, baby girl. Come back to us now. Open your eyes, Princess" I say softly to her.

"Move Pres. Let me look at her" Doc calls out from the doorway. I get up but don't leave her side. Doc shines a light in her eyes and takes her blood pressure. "She has passed out. I have smelling salts in my bag if you want me to wake her" he says to us. I nod my head, and he goes into his bag, pulling out the salts. He waves them under her nose, and Katherine flies up in a fright. She was screaming as she does.

"BUSTER GET IN HERE" I call for Bones' boy. He comes rushing in and comes straight to Katherine. He was calming her down as quick as he can. "It's ok, Princess. I have you, and so does your mum and dad. No one got hurt. I promise you" he whispers to her. She holds onto his cut for dear life. I can see her knuckles turning white with the grip she has on him.

I don't know what it is about him, but he has this calming effect on her that will come in handy. It makes me think that I should have him swap charters and come here. If my Katherine needs him, I will move heaven and hell to get him. I watch Buster and Katherine on the couch together. I watch how gentle he is with her. I should walk away and give her space, but I can't get my feet to move from their spot on the floor.

Buster looks towards me and nods his head, letting me know that Kate has calmed down enough for me to speak to her. I nod my head in thanks back towards him. "Kate?" I call her name. She looks up towards me, and I can see that her eyes are all glossy. I open my arms up wide for her, hoping she will understand that I am no threat to her. Kate takes the opportunity to jump up from the couch and run into my arms. I wrap mine around her extra tight. The tears are falling from Kate's eyes. She pulls back a little and looks at my top. "I'm sorry, Dad," she says to me. I kiss her head.

"Never apologise little one. You can cry on me whenever you want. I will always hold you until your tears have dried up" I tell her with another kiss to her head. Kate rests her head back on my chest.

Diana and Kate have left my office. As Diana has said to me, she needs mother-daughter time with Kate. I didn't want to let her go. Being able to hold my Princess in my arms for the first time in 21 years, has lit a fire in my heart. I never realised how much I needed her and this. From this day forward, I promise to God; I will protect that girl with my whole life.

"Butch, what are we going to do with the problem of your brother and his fuckwits?" Buster asks me. I have no idea what I am going to do, but I know I will kill each and every motherfucker who tries to harm my baby.

"Buster. Can I ask you something?" I question him. Nodding his head in response, I continue. "Would you swap charters if I asked you to stay for Katherine?" I ask. "I'd have to speak to Bones. I am his Enforcer" Buster responds. I grunt in response to him. Making a mental note to ring Bones and tell him the situation.

Walking through the common room, the party has started. Music is thumping throughout. Drinks are being spilt by the old fuckers who can't handle their liquor. "Oi Pres, where's that fine piece of arse you have here now. The boys and I made a bet on who could bed......" his sentence was cut off by my hand around his throat.

"You speak about my daughter like that again, and there will be a bullet in between your eyeballs. Got it cunt?" I scream at him. This cock head nods his head. I drop him with a kick to the ribs as he tries to regain his breath. "That goes for the lot of you. Katherine is not to be touched. She is my daughter. My flesh and blood. She is not a piece of fucking meat for you fuckstains to touch. Got it?" I yell out to the room.

"Yes, Pres" is the only thing I hear from all these fuckers as I continue my walk through the main room. I turn my head to look at Buster, and the look on his face tells me he is ready to kill someone too. I think my baby girl has made an impression on him. I grasp his shoulder. "You have my blessing boy," I tell him. The shocked look on his face tells me he knows what I am talking about.

"Butch, thank you. But it is up to Katherine. I am not going to overstep my mark for her. She needs to come to me" he tells me. I clap him on the shoulder once again. "Still stands, boy," I tell him. There is a sparkle in his eye. I shake my head and chuckle at the boyish behaviour. "Get lost boy. I have a phone call to make" I tell him. He nods his head and makes his way back into the clubhouse.

Taking a seat on the porch, I light up a ciggie and call the person to make all of this happen. After three rings he picks up.

"Bones, I have a favour to ask?" I say to him. "What's up Butch?" He asks me.

"I need your enforcer. I need him here full time" I tell Bones. He umms and ahhs down the line. "This wouldn't have anything to do with that young lady who has just come back into your lives, would it?" Bones asks with a laugh. "Exactly the reason" I respond.

"How does he feel about it?" Bones asks. "He told me he would have to speak to you. Look, if he didn't help my daughter the way he does, I would have sent him on his way back to you. He calms her down when no one can get near her. I need him for her Bones" I plead my case. "Let me throw it to a vote. I'll get back to you with the result" he says. We grunt our goodbyes and hang up.

I continue to sit out on the porch. Lighting another ciggie as soon as I put the first one out. It's loud out here, but it is also tranquil. "What are you doing out here?" comes the sweet voice of my one and only woman. "Come here, Queen," I say to her and grab her hand, bringing her to my lap. "Just enjoying the quietness and the sunset. Thinking how I got so lucky with you as my other-half and an amazing daughter inside" I say to Diana. She leans her head on my shoulder and plants a soft kiss on my cheek.

"We are both pretty lucky. I am just so thankful Katherine is back where she belongs" Diana says to me. We both sit there watching the sunset. My phone pings in my pocket. Pulling it out, I read the text.

"Buster is all yours. Congratulations"

Chapter 8- Joel?

K ate

Spending time with my Mum was terrific. I have longed for this, and I have finally gotten it. The only thing missing right now is, Tracy. I miss her and wish I could call her. I don't know how Mum or Dad would react if I rang her and got her to come here. So much has happened in the past week that I need to destress to her.

"Di...Mum?" I call for Diana. "Yeah, baby?" "Can I please call my friend Tracy? I need to let her know I am safe and okay" I ask her. Hoping that she will let me. "Of course, Princess. Let me grab my phone. I'll be back in a jiffy" she says to me. With a smile, she leaves the room. I stay sitting on the couch in the room. I want to explore, but I am scared of what I may find.

Diana comes back in not five minutes later with her phone. "Here you go, Princess. Take as long as you need" she says to me. Diana places a kiss on my head and leaves the room again. I pull the phone closer to me, staring at the unlocked screen. Pulling up the number pad, I enter in the only phone number I know, apart from my own.

One ring, two rings, three rings. When it gets to the fourth, I pull the phone away from my ear, about to press the end call button when her voice comes through the line. "Hello," Tracy says. "Trace" I whisper out. "Holy shit. Kate? Where the fuck are you?" she screams down the line to me. "I'm safe. I promise." I tell her. "Where are you?" she asks me.

"So, I have some huge news to tell you," I tell her. "What?" she says. "I have sorta found my birth parents" I whisper to her. "What the fuck? Kate, that doesn't answer my question on where the fuck you are" I can tell she is getting annoyed at my avoidance of her questions. "Okay, my Dad and Mum are apart of the Devil's On Wheels MC. I am with them at their base. I am safe. I promise" I tell her. Tracy never makes a sound when I tell her my news.

"Trace, are you there?" I ask her. I check the phone screen to make sure we are still on the line together. "Trace?" still no answer from her. "Tracy for fuck sakes. Will you fucking answer me?" I yell at her. "Do you think they will let me come and see you?" she asks. "Give me a second, and I'll ask," I tell her. Muting the phone call, I leave the room. Spotting Mum and Dad at the bar, I slowly approach them.

"Mum" I call her name. She looks towards me with a big smile. "What's wrong baby?" Mum asks me. "Can my friend come here?" I ask her softly. Diana looks to Butch, and he gives her a slight nod. "Of course she can, baby girl. Your friends are apart of our family" Mum says to me. I smile at both of them and wrap my arms around their shoulders. "Thank you," I tell them and run back to the room I was sitting in.

Taking the phone call off mute, "Trace, pack some shit. You are coming to stay with me." After telling Tracy the rest of the details and letting her know someone will pick her up in a couple of days, I start preparing the room I am staying in for her. There is a soft knock at the door. I approach the door, take a deep breath and slowly open it, to see Buster standing on the other side.

"Hi, Princess," Buster says to me. I give him a small smile and open the door wider for him to come in. He walks in and takes a seat on the chair at my vanity. "What can I do for you, Buster?" I ask him. He just gives me a goofy grin. "Just thought I should let you know that your Dad got me transferred here," Buster says. I look at him in disbelief. "You're staying here now?" I ask him. He nods his head, yes. I don't know what comes over me, but I am throwing myself at him next thing I know—kissing him all over his face.

"Woah, Princess. What's gotten into you?" he asks me—shock written in his eyes. I blush and pull myself back from him, taking a seat on my bed. "I'm sorry," I say to him. I look down at the carpet in the room. Buster walks over to me, as I am now looking at his boots. He bends down in front of me and lifts my chin with his fingers. "I wasn't having a go at you, Princess. I quite enjoyed that, but I was not going to make a move on you until I knew you were on board with me" he whispers to me.

I raise my head to look him in the eyes. "I don't know what it is about you, Buster, but you are the only one I want near me. There is this invisible pull between us" I say to him softly. Buster moves his hands to mine and pulls me up from the bed. As soon as we are both standing, his hands drop to my hips and mine go up and around his neck. "You need to tell me if you don't want this, Katherine. Okay," he says to me. "I want this, and I want you, Buster," I tell him.

Buster slants his lips over mine, pulling me in closer to him by my hips. My breasts are pushed up against his hard chest, our tongues battling for dominance. Buster swings me around and backs me up against the wall in the bedroom. His hands move down from my hips to under my butt cheeks. Hoisting me up, my legs wrapping around his hips. Our mouths never breaking apart. "I am only asking you once more, Katherine. Do you really want this?" Buster asks me after he pulls his mouth away from mine.

I grind myself down on his hard-on, hoping to show him my answer. I grab his face in my hands and smash my lips back onto his, grinding myself more and more. "I need words, Katherine," Buster says to me. "I want this, Buster. Please" I beg him to continue. "You asked for it, baby," Buster says just before he swings us back around and throws me down onto the bed.

I bounce up and down on the mattress a couple of times before Buster has laid himself down on top of me. His mouth ravishes my neck as his hands work on getting my top off me. He unbuttons the flannel shirt, his hands make quick work of my bra. His mouth descends onto my naked breasts. Taking my nipple into his mouth. The moans leaving my mouth, egg him on to keep going.

Buster leans up to start taking his cut off. I stop him with my own hands and then begin to undress him myself. I remove his cut and lay it down on the bed next to us. Next goes his shirt. I sit there, admiring his body. The defined eight pack he has. I lick my lips subconsciously. Buster's eyes follow the movement of my tongue. He pushes me back down onto the mattress and unsnaps my jeans. Pulling them down my legs along with my panties.

Laying on full display for him. I watch him roam his eyes over my body, licking his lips as he does. Without warning, Buster has my legs spread and his face and tongue in my pussy. Licking and sucking on my clit. I am seeing stars. My body is uncontrollably shaking as my orgasm is fast approaching. Buster removes his face and gives me a cheeky grin. "Not yet, Princess," he says to me while unbuttoning his jeans. Pushing them off his hips with his boxers.

He pulls his wallet out of his jeans and removes a condom. "Protection first, Princess," he says to me. Ripping the foil wrapper, he rolls the condom down his shaft and crawls up the bed towards me. My legs wrap around his hips as soon as he gets himself situated. Buster lines his cock up with the opening of my money maker. He slowly slides himself inside of me. The feel of him stretching me, making me moan out.

"Open your eyes, Princess," Buster says to me. I open my eyes and look in his eyes. There is a small smirk on his face. "That's it, baby. Keep your eyes on me. I want to watch the stars in your eyes explode when we do" He says to me. Buster speeds up his movements. My orgasm is starting lowly in my belly. My breathing is coming in short bursts. "Cum now" Buster whispers onto my lips.

Fireworks explode all around me. My orgasm hits me, and it hits hard. This is the first time I have orgasmed because I wanted to. Not because it was demanded of me. Buster thrust a couple more times, to bring us down from our orgasms. He kisses me passionately. "You're mine now, Princess" he whispers into my ear. The smile could not be wiped from my face.

Buster rolls off me and lays next to me, wrapping his arms around me. "Buster?" I call him. "Joel," he says to me. "Huh?" I look at him, confused. "My name is Joel. You will call me Joel from now on, Princess" he says to me. "Well, Joel. Hi." I say to him with a giggle. Joel smiles at me, a real genuine, toothy smile. "Hi, Princess," he says back to me. Blush rises up my cheeks.

Our moment is interrupted by a knock at the door. The person doesn't wait for us to speak before they walk in. "Holy shit. Put some fucking clothes on" Dad screams out. Joel quickly jumps on top of me to cover me from my Dad. "Maybe next time you should wait for me to say enter before walking in Dad" I yell at him. Dad closes the door with him on the other side. "Put some clothes on and join us in the common room for a meal you two. Fuck. I need to bleach my fucking eyeballs" he cries out, walking down the hallway.

I look up at Joel and start laughing. "Come on, Princess. Let's go shower before dinner" Joel says. He helps me up from the bed, and we enter the bathroom that is attached to my room. He starts the water and pushes me into the cubicle, closing the door behind himself. "Round 2?" he whispers into my ear. I feel my body relax into his arms. Joel pushes me into the wall. My breast are pressed against the cool tiles.

Joel grabs my hips and pulls them back to arch my back. He doesn't take me gently, and I am coming quicker than before, but I wouldn't have it any other way. He helps me clean up afterwards. I quickly get dressed into the jeans and bra I was wearing before. I went without my panties as I don't have any other clean ones here. Buttoning up my flannel shirt, Diana knocks on the door. "Just making sure you guys were coming down for dinner," she says to us.

Joel looks at me and then back to my Mum. "Yes, ma'am. We will be there in a moment" he says to her. She smiles at us and closes the door behind her. As soon as I am dressed, Joel grabs my hand and leads me out of the room and down the stairs. Getting to the bottom of the stairs, there is hooting and hollering. "Congrats, Buster. Got yourself a good chick there" Dad's VP, Raider, calls out. Joel smiles at them and then at me, giving me a quick kiss on my lips.

The hooting and hollering continue, beers being passed around to everyone. One of the women offers me one, and I shake my head no. "No, thank you," I say to her. She keeps passing out the beers to all of them in the common room. Food is being brought out by both the guys and girls of the club.

Dad stands up and whistles out to get everyone's attention.

"Just a quick speech. Buster here has claimed my baby girl as his Old Lady. Everyone raise your glasses for these two sickos" Dad finishes his speech. Beer bottles clink together, and all the members let out whistles. The party for the night lasts until the very late hours of the next morning. I tried my hardest to stay awake, but I could feel my eyes getting heavy around 3:30 am.

"I'm taking my woman to bed," Joel tells the room. "No one disturb us," he says that while looking directly at my Dad. Dad raises his hands in a surrender motion. "Lock the door next time" is all that Dad says to us. Joel smiles at him, picks me up and carries me up the stairs into my room. He gently lays me in the bed and climbs in next to me. "Sweet sleep, Princess" Joel whispers to me and kisses my forehead, before the darkness consumes me.

Chapter 9- Tracy arrives

K ate

It's been four days since I spoke with Tracy. Mum and Dad sent Savage to get her from her house and bring her back here. They should be arriving anytime now. I keep pacing the common room floor, looking out the windows for them to arrive. "Princess, you need to sit down," Joel says to me. I shake my head at him and continue pacing back and forth.

"Kate, if you do not sit down, I will force you to sit down and then I will hold you down," Joel tells me. I look at him, with my mouth open. "You wouldn't dare to," I say to him. He looks up at me, with a wicked grin on his face. "Try me, Princess." He says to me. I start moving back towards the clubhouse doors. "You'll have to catch me first," I tell him turning around and taking off outside.

The rain is pouring and hitting the gravel hard. The heavy downpour is flicking up little stones. I run down off the porch into the grassy area. I'm stopped when I heard noises coming from the south end of the property. The noises are not the usual bikes, but what sounds like trucks of some sort. I turn around to run back in when a gunshot goes off. I hit the ground and cover my head.

I start screaming at the noise, hoping my voice can be heard over the rain. "HELP" I scream out. I start crawling towards the clubhouse doors when something grabs my ankle. "Where are you going you little whore?" the voice from my nightmares asks me. I use my other foot to kick them in the face. His hold on me releases, and I can jump up quickly and get to the clubhouse doors.

Joel takes one look at me when I get the door open, and he is on his feet quickly. "Kate?" he calls my name. I drop to my knees, breathing heavily. "Kate, what happened?" He asks me. I don't have the time to answer when gunshots ring out through the clubhouse doors. "FUCK" Joel yells out. He drags me away from the clubhouse doors further into the common room.

He pulls me into behind the booths and tells me to stay low. "Babe, I won't be long okay. I will get rid of the fuckers, and I will be back for you. I promise" Joel says to me. By this time, I am able to mutter out a few words. "John," I tell Joel. He nods his head, pulls out his gun, screams for my Dad and slowly walks towards the clubhouse doors.

A massive explosion goes off as soon as Joel had made it to the door. "JOELLLLLLLLLLLLL" I scream. I am trying to look around the other guys. Raider grabs me and holds me to his chest. "Calm down, Kate. I need you to calm down" he says to me. My body goes into shock and panic. My eyes are roaming the doors to the clubhouse, looking around for Joel. "Joel" I keep calling his name, with no response from him.

"DOC" I hear my Dad call out. "Get down here now. We need immediate medical attention" he calls out after Doc made himself known. I keep trying to get up to see where Joel is, but Raider firmly holds on me. "Kate, please, I am begging you not to fight me right now. I need you to stay down" Raider whispers into my ear. I clutch his cut in my hands, feeling my tears soaking my face.

"Keep her down and out of view" Dad calls out to the room. I know exactly who he is talking about. More of the men come forward to block my view of what is going on. Joel has been moved into another room, and I am left on the floor alone. As soon as the room's door was shut, Raider got up and left me on the floor in my own panic.

My vision starts to blur. My breathing is ragged. I cannot get a deep breath in. My chest is constricting so much that the room begins to spin. "AHHHHHHHH" I scream out before the darkness consumes me.

I slowly start coming back to the land of the living, when I hear the voice, I have been missing. "Where the fuck is she?" Tracy screams out. I raise my hand from my position on the floor. "What the fuck are you doing on the floor?" Tracy says to me as she rushes to me. She picks me up and holds me to her. "I have been so worried about you, Kate. What has happened?" Tracy asks me while rocking my body with hers.

"Where do I start?" I ask her. "From the beginning," she says. "I sit there and tell her everything that has happened in the past week and a half. Tracy sat there and never said a word. She took everything in. "So, one of the guys who saved you after you ran away from me, is now living here and you are his?" she asks me. I nod my head, yes, to answer her question. "And he was the one who got injured and then everyone left you alone?" I nod my head again.

"I'm going to fucking kill them all. What a bunch of dumb cunts" Tracy says, anger lacing her voice. "Don't start trouble young lady" a male voice speaks to her. She looks up and smiles at my Dad's Sergeant at Arms. "Sorry, Savage, but her man gets injured and they keep her away and then once he is safe in the other room every fucking person gets up and leaves her like she is meant to be able to manage this shit on her own. I am fucking fuming right now" Tracy tells him. He just looks at her and then at me then back to her.

"They left you?" he asks me. I nod my head, yes. "Who was it?" he asks. "Raider," I tell him. His eyes flash with anger. "RAIDER" Savage screams out. Raider comes from another room. "What the fuck is your problem now, Sav?" Raider asks. "Are you fucking serious right now? You know Kate does not handle stressful situations, and then you fuck off when she needs someone the most. Just wait till I tell Butch" Savage says. Raider takes a step towards Savage. "Go ahead, boy. I'll deny everything" Raider says.

I stand up on shaky legs and head towards the hallway. I need to find Joel to make sure he is okay. "Kate" Tracy calls for me. I ignore her calls and keep moving towards the rooms. I open every door that I come across, all coming up empty. The last door on the left is locked, but I can hear voices coming from the other side. I knock on the door.

The door opens slowly, and my Dad's head pokes out. "Kate, please, you need to walk away," he says to me. I stand there with tears falling down my cheeks. "NO" I scream at him. "I need to see him," I tell him. He opens the door a little wider. I go to move to step in, but Dad stops me by stepping out of the room. He closes the door behind himself.

"Kate, Buster is badly injured. He took the full brunt of the explosion. He isn't missing body parts as such, but he has cuts and abrasions all over his body. You do not need to see him." Dad says to me. My body is shaking, my legs give out from under me, and I hit the wall behind me. Dad steps forward and grabs me in his arms, holding me to his chest. "Princess, he will be okay. I promise. But right now, you don't need to see him like this" Dad says to me.

He picks me up and carries me out towards the common room. "I don't want to be out there" I whisper to him. He nods his head and turns around for the stairs and carries me up to my room. Laying me on my bed, he plants a kiss to my forehead. "I'm sorry baby girl. But once he is awake and cleaned up, I will take you to see him" Dad whispers to me. I blink up at him and then roll over hugging myself around my waist, letting the tears and heartache show.

I could hear Tracy still yelling at everyone in the common room. Telling them all how much they are a bunch of gutless pigs. Leaving a defenceless girl on the floor to have who knows what happened to her. Dad's voice bellows through the building, yelling out "Who the fuck is this little red-head?" I know Tracy won't stand for that. I untangle myself from myself and get out of bed. Opening my door, I yell at the top of my lungs.

"TRACY, GET YOUR ARSE UP THESE STAIRS AND COME HOLD ME" I yell down to her. "About time I heard her voice again" Tracy calls out, running up the stairs. She makes it to my floor and runs straight into my waiting arms. "Come on, Katie-poo. Let's take a nap" she says with a wink. More footsteps can be heard on the stairs, and Savage comes into sight. "If there is any girl on girl action happening, I want in," he says with a wicked smirk.

Tracy flips him off and pushes me into my room, slamming the door shut behind us. We look at each other and start laughing. I am past the point of just laughing when no noise is coming out of my mouth, and I can't seem to take a breath in. Tracy pats my back and blows in my face. "There bitch, now fucking breath you wanker" she says to me with a smile.

We lay down on the bed together and get comfortable. Tracy is the big spoon, holding me close to her chest. "I fucked Savage on the way here" she whispers into my ear. I roll over, so we are nose to nose. "Was it good?" I ask her. "The best I've ever had. He was rough and gentle at the same time. I think I would very happily be fucked by him again and again" she says back with a twinkle in her eye. I send her a smile. I am happy for her, but then I think about Joel, and the smile is wiped from my face, and the tears fill my eyes again.

Tracy notices the change in my mood and holds me tighter to her. "He will be okay. You will be laying with him in no time, Kate." Tracy says to me, kissing my head. "Dad wouldn't even let me see him. I just need to know he is okay and I just want to hold his hand and kiss his face, and, and, and......." "Shhhh, Katie. You will be able to soon. Is that old scary motherfucker out there your Dad?" Tracy asks. I nod my head and giggle a little.

"I think I pissed him off with all my yelling," she says with a smirk. "He'll learn to love you," I tell her. She nods her head and gets another twinkle in her eye. This one tells me she is coming up with ideas on how to piss my Dad off more. "Stop it, Tracy. He will not be afraid to hurt you. Please stop playing with fire" I beg her. She gives me a small smile, and I can tell she is thinking over my words. "I can't promise you anything, but I will give it my best shot," she says. I nod my head and close my eyes, letting sleep take over me.

I wake during the middle of the night. Tracy is no longer in my bed, only one guess where she is? I quietly tiptoe out of my room and down the stairs. I reach the hallway where Joel is. Moving towards the door, I turn the handle and find it is unlocked. I open the door slowly and poke my head in. Joel is laying on the bed in there, asleep. He is hooked up to different machines. I tiptoe over to his bed after shutting the door behind me.

I quietly and softly get onto the bed next to him, laying my head on his chest. I close my eyes and listen to the steady rhythm of his heartbeat. It lulls me into a sense of security and allows me to fall asleep. Holding the man that is slowly but surely stealing my heart.

I'm woken only a few hours later by voices whispering around me. "Should we move her?" "Nah let her sleep. She needs to be with him" "I need to check him out but I can't with her laying on him" I open my eyes and turn my head to look at who was in the room. "Sorry, Doc," I say to him. I gently lift myself off of Joel's chest. I am about to climb off the bed when a hand grips my wrist. I turn my head and look Joel in the eyes. He gives me a small smile.

My body relaxes at seeing Joel's eyes and his smile. "Welcome back," Doc says from behind me. "Let me do a couple of quick checks, and then I'll leave ya alone with ya woman," Doc says. Joel nods his head at Doc and then looks back to me. "I'm just going to get some water. I will be back" I tell him. Joel smiles at me again. He brings my wrist up to his face and places a gentle kiss on the inside of my wrist and then lets me go.

I jump off the bed and run out of the door. I make it to the kitchen in under a minute, grabbing a bottle of water from the fridge and getting one for Joel. I didn't realise I had a smile on my face until Mum points it out. "What's got you smiling so big this morning?" she asks me. I turn to her, "Joel's awake" I squeak out. Her smile widens to be the same size as mine. "Oh thank god," Mum says. "Go baby girl. Go get your man" she tells me. I smile once more at her and take off back to the room he is in.

Nothing can wipe the smile off my face today.

Chapter 10

R aider

Ever since that stupid little girl has come back, everything is about her and her needs. After Buster was blown up, just a pity it didn't kill him, I left her on the floor in her panic attack. With the hope that it would kill her, I left her there to die. To my surprise, the little bitch woke up. "I need to inform John" I whisper to myself as I sit in the common room by myself drinking a beer.

Butch comes in and takes a seat at the table with me. "What's up with you lately?" Butch asks me. "Nothing. Just trying to come to terms with Katherine being back and all" I tell him, lying through my teeth. "It's fucking amazing that she is back. I had started to think she was dead" Butch tells me. "Wish she was" I whisper under my breath. Thankfully Butch didn't hear me.

My phone rings in my pocket. I pull it out and see John's name on the screen. "I gotta take this," I tell Butch as I get up and walk out the club-house.

"Hello" I answer the phone. "How much damage was done?" John asks. "Just the front door and Katherine's fuck buddy was hurt but not fatally. She suffered a panic attack. She didn't die, unfortunately," I tell him. "Nah, I don't want a panic attack to take her. I want to string her by her ankles and gut her like my Jane was" John says to me down the line.

"Next time she is alone I'll let you know. I will try and get her by herself as soon as I can, but she has extra protection at the moment" I tell him. John grunts and hangs up on me. I put my phone back in my jeans pocket and pull out a ciggie. Lighting it up and sucking it down, I think about the next time I can get that stupid little bitch by herself. I want Butch and Diana to hurt. They hurt me twenty-five years ago when they introduced John to Jane.

Jane was my woman. We were going to be together. I just had to wait for her to become of legal age. But as soon as she turned 18, Butch pushed John towards her, and they fell in love. She was with him for three years when she was murdered. Jane was strung up by her ankles and gutted like a fish. The only problem with that was, one of the club's prospects caught the killer in the act, and the killer could only do the one thing he had to. Kill the prospect.

Leaving the prospects vest at the scene was my best idea yet. If I couldn't have Jane, no one could. Yes, that's right. I killed Jane. I was so in love with her, and she turned her back on me and chose John. I bided my time and took her when they were at their happiest. She was just pregnant with their first child. I took her, drug her, fucked her and then killed her. Blaming Butch's club the whole time.

I know, I'm a sick fuck, but as I have said. If I couldn't have her, no one could. But this little bit of information will be taken to the grave with me. No one will know the truth, and especially after Katherine is murdered, I will be home scott free.

I am brought out of my own head when a hand lands on my shoulder. I turn my head to look at who the hand belongs to. "Here, this is from John," Brad says to me. I take the envelope from him and nod my head. Brad takes off again into the woods behind the compound. I hide the envelope in the front of my jeans, pulling my top and cut down over the top of it.

I walk back into the clubhouse straight to the stairs that lead to the bedrooms. Walking up the stairs, Savage hits me with his shoulder. Fucking dickhead, thinks I am scared of him. I have killed more people in this world than he has, so his 'threatening' looks don't do shit for me. I make it to the top floor and enter my room. I pull the envelope out of my jeans and rip it open, pulling out the paper on the inside.

Pete,

We need to get Katherine alone, and we need to do it soon. If you can't get her to be alone for me to grab, maybe you could do it for me. Hide her somewhere no one will find her, and then I will reward you at the end of it.

If you are up to it, I need Butch and Diana gone too. You are closer to them than I am, so maybe you could help with ending their lives as well as their stupid whore of a daughter.

Let me know what you think?

John

I read his letter over and over and can feel my blood boiling. That cunt wants me to do all his dirty work. I will help him with Katherine, but that is as far as it goes.

I rip the letter up and throw it in the bin in my bathroom. I will help get Katherine, but the rest, John can do the rest himself. I leave my room and head back down the stairs to the bar. I need a few more beers tonight. I grab two bottles and take them outside. I sit on the picnic table in the yard, sinking back the cold beer when Butch approaches me.

"What the fuck is going on with you, Raider?" Butch asks me as he sits down. I shake my head at him, telling him nothing and to leave it. Butch being Butch, doesn't know how to leave shit alone. "Nah, mate. Fucking tell me" he demands. I can feel my blood pressure rising and the heat from the anger filling my veins.

"You want to know what the fuck is going on? Well, I'll fucking tell you. Ever since that slut of a daughter of yours walked back into your fucking life, you changed. You are no longer the brutal motherfucker I have ever met. You are a soft cunt, and it is not something that I can handle. She has made you weak" I yell at my Pres. I can see the anger in his eyes at what I have just said, but he wanted to know the fucking truth.

Butch stands up from where he was sitting. I can tell he is pinching the bridge of his nose. "What the fuck is your problem with my daughter Raider? Are you more upset with the fact you can't fuck her like you fuck every other woman that walks in the fucking clubhouse doors?" Butch yells at me without looking at me.

"Go fuck yourself, Butch. Your daughter is used. She was fucking raped by your brother and his fucking stepson. I wouldn't touch her with a fucking ten-foot pole. Who the fuck knows what diseases she fucking has. I bet once she got away from them, she turned into a fucking prostitute. I would be keeping a closer eye on her. She will burn through all the boys in that clubhouse, and once she is done, she will run away for her new fix" I yell back at Butch.

I didn't see it coming, but I am now laid out on the floor. My cheek and jaw are killing me. "Don't you ever speak about my daughter like that again. You are walking a very fine line Raider, and I will not hesitate to kick your arse out of here" Butch yells at me then turns around and walks away. I stay laying on the ground, closing my eyes and breathing heavily through my nose.

I slowly drag myself up off the ground and grab my second bottle of beer, taking a massive gulp. I do not regret anything I have done or said in my life, and I will not start. His daughter is a hindrance in this place. She needs to go, and it needs to be done quickly. The more she is around here, the more likely the truth will come out, and I cannot afford for that to happen.

I throw my now empty bottle of beer on the ground and get up, heading back towards the clubhouse. I make it to the door and take a deep breath before opening it and walking in. The room goes quiet when I walk in. I take note of all their eyes. A lot of them have looks of anger and others of pity. I keep moving towards the stairs and take them two at a time.

Reaching my room, I open the door and slam it behind me. I know I have fucked up, but I don't regret it. I do not need to regret anything. All I know is that what I have done will come to the grave at the end of the day with me.

Kate

The clubhouse has a really weird vibe tonight. I don't know what has happened, but I don't think it is good. I approach Mum to see if she will tell me what has happened. I wrap my arms around her waist from behind and rest my head on her back. "Hi, Princess" Mum says to me. I can tell something is up with the tone of her voice.

"What have I missed?" I ask her. Mum shakes her head and zips her lips. At the sight of that, I know something has been said about me. I didn't want this to happen, with me coming back. I untangle my arms from around her waist and give her a quick kiss on her head. "Okay, then. I'm just gonna go find Trace now" I tell her.

I walk away from Mum, making it look like I am looking around for the room for Tracy. Instead of going to find her, I head towards the stairs. Me being here is only going to cause problems. Joel has been hurt because of me. Dad and his club are on alert all the time. I think it is time I turn around and leave. Even though I know, I have only ever wanted to be apart of a family, but if me being here is going to cause issues, I am better off not being here.

I quickly pack a bag and throw it out the window. I am going to head out through the back door. I quietly leave the bedroom and head down the stairs. The mood is still sombre. Thankfully, no one watches me come down the stairs. I turn down the hallway, towards the back door of the club. I open the door and head out, walking around the side of the building, grabbing my bag.

Walking towards the road, I make it outside the compound without being seen and head off down the road. I know this was a mistake. I know now that everything I do only cause issues for the people around me. I hope they will forgive me, but to keep everyone safe, I am out of there.

Daylight starts breaking over the small town where Dad and Mum live. I made it to the city centre, but now I need to rest. My legs are killing me, and my stomach is growling for food. Patting my pockets, I don't feel my wallet. "Fuck" I whisper to myself. I left my phone at the clubhouse so they couldn't track me, but I forgot to grab my wallet. I quickly check my bag in case I put it in there.

Nothing. "Shit, fuck, shit," I say to myself. "Are you ok, dear?" an older lady asks me. "Mmhmm. I'm fine. Thank you for asking" I say to her, hoping she will get the hint and walk away. She smiles at me "You don't look fine. Did you need some money?" she asks me. My mouth hangs open at her question. "How did you know?" I whisper to her. "I saw you pat yourself down and then check your bag. I don't have a lot, but I will be happy to get you a meal" she tells me.

I throw my arms around this lovely lady. "Thank you so much. I have been walking all night" I tell her. She smiles and links her arm with mine and steers me towards a small diner. Sitting at the table, I order a small meal. She looks at me strangely but doesn't question me. The food comes out, and I eat mine slowly. I am trying to saviour the flavour. This will be my last meal for a while.

When the plates had been cleared, I stood up and gave the lovely lady another hug and thanked her again and again. She just kept smiling at me. I picked up my bag and gave her a small smile, heading towards the door to the diner. My breath caught in my throat when I see John and Brad walking down the street towards this diner.

I quickly turn around and look for a back exit. The lady is still standing where I left her, but this time when I look at her, her small smile has turned into an evil grin. "Goodbye, Katherine," she says. Pain runs through my head, and all I see is the ground getting closer to my face before the lights are turned off.

Chapter 11- Is the end near?

✱ ***Trigger Warning****

This chapter mentions sexual assault. If this subject is to cause any harm to you please do not read. Read at your own discretion

Butch

Everything in this club is going to shit lately. No, it isn't because Kate is back. It is because there are members of this club who think standing up to me is going to win them brownie points with others. Not on my watch will anybody here disrespect me, my wife or my daughter. I am sick to fucking death of people assuming that what they say is correct and everything I do is wrong.

The whole clubhouse is quiet tonight. No rowdy parties, no swinging from the chandeliers. Nothing. Just a sour mood and I am feeling it the most—my best friend. The only man I would class as blood family in this club treats my own flesh and blood like shit. Like she isn't worth our time.

Raider, he knows he has fucked up, but by the look on his face, he doesn't care. My blood is boiling. I am ready to rip his fucking face off. No one talks shit about my daughter like that. NO ONE. I watch my Princess come out of the hallway from Buster's room and go straight to her Mum. I have told everyone to not say anything to her about what has happened.

I watch her with Diana. I can't see what they are talking about, but she must be asking about what has happened. Diana zips her lips, and I can see the defeat in Katherine's eyes. "Butch, what are you going to do with Raider?" Savage asks me as he walks up to my table. "No fucking idea, Sav. I don't know what Kate has done to him" I tell him.

I look back over towards Diana and see she is on her own. I do a quick scan of the room and can't she Kate anywhere. Thinking she has gone back to Buster, I continue my conversation with Savage. "I do have to tell you when Buster was hurt; Raider was with Katherine. He could tell she was going into a panic attack, but as soon as Buster was out of sight, he just left her there" Savage tells me.

My head whips to his quick smart. "What the fuck did you just say?" I ask him. My voice raising after every word. Savage repeats what he has just said to me and all I see is red. I stand up from my chair and flip the table over. "HE FUCKING LEFT HER ALONE WHILE SHE WAS HAVING AN ATTACK" I yell out. The whole room turns to look at me. Savage puts his hand on my shoulder to try and calm me down. Diana makes her way over to me also.

"That piece of shit left her to suffer alone," I tell Diana. She wraps her arms around me and rests her head on my chest. "Don't let it get you worked up. Just breath for me okay" Diana tells me. I wrap my arms around her and rest my cheek on her head. I watch the little redhead, who I came to know as Kate's friend Tracy, say something to Savage. He nods his head, and she heads off to the stairs.

Savage picks up the table and places it back where it belongs. A minute later, Tracy comes running down the stairs. "Kate's gone. She has left her phone and wallet, but she is not anywhere upstairs" she calls out. I get up and move down the hallway to Buster's room. I open the door and see him in there with Doc.

"Kate in here?" I ask them. Both of them shake their heads no. I run back out to the common room. Everyone had started looking for her, but come up empty. "FUCK" I yell out. My fucking Princess is gone again from right under our fucking noses.

"Buster, you are going to rip all your fucking stitches. Get back into the fucking bed" I hear Doc yell out. Buster comes storming into the common room. "Where the fuck is she?" he yells out. None of us could answer him. "Where the fuck has she gone? Who fucked with her?" he yells out. No one makes a sound. He looks like a raging bull ready to headbutt anyone who gets in his fucking way.

I spend most of my night in my office going over maps on where she could have gotten to. I have sent guys out in all directions looking for her. She couldn't have gotten far in the amount of time she has been gone. I swear I didn't see her for 10 fucking minutes.

I drag my hand down my face and take notice that the sun has risen. There have been no sightings of Kate anywhere, and the guys have been out most of the night. Diana has shut down again like she did twenty-one years ago. Buster is on the edge of a dangerous place. I have been there and know the signs, but I know he needs to be on the edge for a little bit longer before I pull him back from the end.

I stand up and look out my office window. Guys are riding back in and swapping with others. They must be discussing where they have looked and where else to go. I am starting to grow impatient by this stage. Where the fuck is my daughter? And how the fuck did she get out of here unseen?

I head into the common room, and the place is quiet. Most of the guys are still looking at maps of the area, here and where she came from. A prospect comes barging into the room from the main doors. "PRES" he yells out. I look at him and raise my eyebrow. "Unmarked truck drove by, and threw this out of the window. Didn't get a good look at them as they had their faces covered. Sav and Skulls went after them" the prospect spits out.

I pick up the item that was thrown—a CD in a cover. I open the lid and inside is a note that reads 'Watch me'. I don't waste any time and throw the CD into the DVD player at the bar. The picture comes up grainy. I can't see or hear anything until a light comes on. There in the middle of the screen is my girl, tied down to a table. She is as naked as the day she was born.

John and Brad then make themselves known on the video. They walk over to Katherine's naked body. She is unconscious. I can already feel my blood starting to boil. John opens his mouth to speak. "Hello brother. Look who I have here. She is such a pretty little thing. Guess what brother? I am going to fuck your daughter so fucking hard that she will never walk again. And while I am fucking her tight pussy, Brad here will ram his massive cock down her throat. The poor girl will never speak again and walk again. So much fun to be had"

I can feel the blood draining from my face. My little brother and his fucked up step-son have my baby. My own flesh and blood and are going to hurt her. I know I shouldn't keep watching, but I need to know what they do to my baby so that I can do it back to them. I hear what sounds like a belt buckle hitting the floor when a loud gunshot comes through the TV screen. Both the fucks run from the room, leaving the video rolling.

Another masked figure comes into screen and undoes the cuffs on Kate's arms and legs. "I will protect you as much as I can," it says. It's voice letting us know it is male. He picks up her naked body and throws her over his shoulder. "Let's get you dressed and out of here," he says to her. The video keeps rolling, and the next sound is John screaming "where the fuck is she?"

The video cuts out. I am on the floor on my hands and knees. Tears are falling down my face. My baby is stuck with those things, and no one here knows where she is. I sit back on my heels and watch as my VP comes down the stairs. He has not once gone out and looked for Kate, but I don't expect him to. He looks at me, with a look I cannot decipher. I stare back at him with no emotions on my face.

I have nothing to say to him, and right now, my mind is on finding my daughter and bringing her back home.

Kate

My shivering body wakes me up from the nightmare I was having. My head is pounding, and my arms and legs feel like jelly. I blink my eyes a few times, adjusting to the light that is shining down on me. Except it isn't just a light, but the sun. I look down at my body and notice I am naked. The harsh wind blows once again, sending shivers through my body.

I muster all the strength I have and push myself into a sitting position. I cover my chest with my arms as best I can. I don't see anything around me apart from trees and grass. I am in an open field of just nature. "Hello" I call out. Hoping someone will hear me. "Is anyone there?" I try it again. My mind is racing on what the hell has happened.

I ran from the clubhouse, met an old lady, she fed me and then, nothing. I can't remember a fucking thing after that. What the fuck happened? I question myself. In the distance, I can hear motorcycles being revved. Trying to pull myself up onto my feet, I slip and go back down. Knowing that is useless, I try to crawl. My body is weak from not having anything to eat or drink for who knows how long.

I crawl as far as I can before I have to stop. The tears are flowing down my cheeks. My hands and knees are cut up from all the twigs and stones on the ground. I scream as loud as I can. All that does is makes the birds fly out of the trees. I lay down on my side and curl up into a ball, sobbing. Not knowing where I am and who did this to me, is making my brain malfunction.

I must have fallen asleep as a wet nose on my face is waking me up. I slowly open my eyes and come face to face with an animal. Shocked out of my sleepy haze, I look into the eyes of the dog in front of me. Slowly raising my clenched fist in front of its face, I wait for it to sniff my hand. When it does, I gently pat it between its ears. "Where are your owners?" I ask the dog, knowing it cannot answer me.

The dog barks at me and starts chasing its own tail. I giggle a little at its bizarre behaviour. "Frankie. Where are you, boy?" comes the female voice. "Frankie" she screams again. Frankie, who must be the dog, starts barking for its owner. I can hear the footsteps coming closer. She must be running. "Frankie what are you...." Her words are stopped short when she sees me.

"Holy shit. Are you Kate?" she asks me. I nod my head at her. She pulls her phone out of her pocket and quickly types into the screen. Pulling the phone to her ear, "Skulls, I have her. She is in the field not far from the compound on the east side. Bring Diana and clothes, blankets and water" she yells down the line. She then turns back to me with a smile on her face.

"Hi, Princess. I'm Daisy, but they call me Whipper" she says. I smile the best smile I can back at her, even though it must look like a grimace. "Oh, Kate, stop ok. They will be here with warmth for you" she says to me while sitting down and pulling my body close to hers. "Do you know what happened?" Daisy asks me. I shake my head no at her. I only know the small parts of what happened, but that is all.

More footsteps can be heard, and it sounds like a herd of elephants running towards us. In front of all the people is Mum. She gets to us first with blankets in her arms. She throws the blankets at Daisy and then throws her arms around me. Daisy places the blankets around my shoulders while Mum holds me tightly to her chest.

I hear a car engine approaching us slowly. I look up and sitting in the driver's seat is Dad, and next to him is my Joel. They both have relieved looks on their faces to see me. Dad jumps out as soon as the car is parked and runs over to us. Sitting behind me, he throws his arms around both Mum and me. We must sit there for a while, as my butt is numb. Dad stands first and helps Mum up. He then picks me up, wrapped in the blanket and carries me to the car.

No words are spoken between us. Dad places me in the backseat. Joel had moved from the front seat to the back and is now holding me to him. His body heat is warming me up both on the inside and the out. Joel holds me to him in a tight hold. Probably scared that I am going to run away again. Still, no words are spoken. The drive back to the compound is the quietest ride I have ever been in.

As soon as the car was parked, Joel jumped out and allowed my Dad to pick me up again. Another blanket was thrown over me, and I was carried into the clubhouse via the main doors, up the stairs into my bedroom. Dad places me on the bed, kisses my forehead and walks out. I can already feel the tears falling from my eyes, knowing I have disappointed him.

Mum comes in with a small smile. "I made you a warm tea. Drink that up and get some rest, beautiful" she says to me, handing me the cup of tea. I take it from her with a small thanks and take a sip. The warmth of the tea is heating up my insides. I still sit on the bed with tears falling down my cheeks. Mum sighs and leaves the room. I am once again left on my own to try and work out what the hell happened.

Chapter 12- The calm before the storm.

K ate

A couple of months have passed since the last time I had seen John or Brad. I was not allowed out of the clubhouse for an entire month. I was grounded. It actually was the most fantastic thing to have been. Joel has been very quiet towards me. He still sleeps next to me of a night time, but that is about it. He barely looks at me when we are in the bar together. I need to pick up my big girl knickers and find out what the fuck everyone is keeping from me.

I walk into the common room, and the room goes silent. This has been happening ever since I got back here. I walk with my head held high and spot my Dad across the room. He looks at me once and then turns his head and continues his talk with whoever is there with him. I walk straight to the bar and grab a bottle of whiskey. Unscrewing the cap, I take mouthful of the amber liquid after mouthful. My throat is burning from the whiskey, but I continue on, not letting it affect me.

Mum sees me and tries to snatch the bottle from my grasp. I look at her and growl. "Don't" I tell her. She tries to turn on the angry face that she has and goes to snatch it again. I turn my whole body away from her. "I said, don't. No one will talk to me here so I may as well write myself off every fucking night until some fucker has the balls to tell me what the fuck happened" I yell at her and walk away.

"KATHERINE" my Dad calls my name. I stop and turn to look at him. "NEVER AND I MEAN NEVER SPEAK TO YOUR MOTHER THAT WAY" he spits at me. I roll my eyes, turn my back and continue walking away. It's ok for everyone here to not talk to me, but the minute I get my back up, I'm the bad person. Well, fuck them.

I enter my room, slamming my door behind me, even though it doesn't bang shut. Because I was in my head, I never heard the footsteps behind me. "Seriously, Kate? What the fuck is going on with you?" Joel asks me. I look at him with hurt in my eyes. "Why would you fucking care, Joel? You never talk to me to find out what is going on, and you never tell me what the fuck happened?" I spit at him. Taking another swig of the whiskey, Joel comes forward and snatches the bottle from my hands.

"What the fuck, Joel?" I scream at him. "ENOUGH" he yells back at me. "You want to know what the fuck happened when you ran?" he asks me. I nod my head, yes. "Your father was sent a video, and in that video, you were naked and unconscious on a fucking table. John and Brad were going to fucking rape you" Joel tells me. I can taste the bile rising in the back of my throat. I swallow it down and try to remain calm.

"Your father watched as you were going to be sexually assaulted. Now you know why everyone is walking around on fucking eggshells with you. No one knows how to fucking act" he spits out. My blood is boiling. Is that why no one speaks to me? Including my fucking parents. I look towards Joel, "Get out" I yell at him. "Get the fuck out of my room and out of my fucking life. You act like you want me but when push comes to shove you treat me like a fucking child. Well, sor-ry I am not a fucking perfect little angel. It wasn't my fault I was raised like a whore" I scream at him.

I turn my back on him and storm into the bathroom. Slamming the door behind me. I leaned back on the door and slid down it to sit on my arse. Now I know why no one speaks to me. Now I know that they all think I am made of glass. My tears are spilling down my cheeks. I can feel my heart rate increasing. I know I am about to have a panic attack, and usually, this is where I will try and control my breathing, but fuck it. No one out there cares about me so who cares if this panic attack kills me. Everyone would be better off without me around.

I can feel my body being slid across the cold floor. Not knowing where I am, I scream at the top of my lungs. "Fuck, Princess. What the hell are you doing on the floor?" I hear the gruff voice of my Dad. "Wishing I was dead," I tell him with no emotion in my voice. He squeezes in the small gap of the doorway and sits down on the floor next to my laying body.

"I'm sorry I never told you what had happened, Kate. But some things you just don't need to know" Dad tells me. "Save it for someone who actually cares. Not one person out there had the guts to tell me what the hell happened. It took me to start losing myself before someone spoke up. How do you think it makes me feel knowing everyone out there walked on eggshells, huh?" I ask him. Dad can't even look me in the face by this point.

"Exactly as I thought. Just let me walk away from here. No one will miss me" I tell him. I am past the point of caring anymore. I thought being reunited with my family would bring me closure to that part of my life, but it has done the opposite. I am still treated like shit. Except for this time, I am not a sex slave, I am just ignored and forgotten about.

Dad gets up the leaves the bathroom. I kick the door closed with my foot, making sure it slams hard with the force I kicked it. I stay in the same position Dad found me in. Not a care in the fucking world to move. Mum, Joel, Tracy and even Savage all come up to try and get me to move. They all were told the same thing. "Fuck off and leave me alone". I know I must be acting like a child, but fuck them. They want to treat me like one, I will act like one.

The bass from the music being played in the common room is making the bathroom floor vibrate. I pull myself up off the floor and enter the bedroom. The room is in darkness. I find the light switch and turn it on. In my head, I am telling myself to pack my shit again and this time don't forget my money. I walk to my cupboard and grab my duffle bag out. I throw it onto my bed and start placing clothes into it.

I grab everything that I need, leaving the rest here. I zip my bag up once it was filled and grab my phone and wallet. Patting my pockets to make sure I have everything, I leave the bedroom. I walk down the stairs and can hear the club having the time of their lives. Getting the courage, I walk through the common room once I make to the bottom of the stairs. I am going to leave with them all watching me.

With my hand on the door, someone grabs my elbow and swings me back towards them. "Where are you going?" I look up and into the eyes of Joel. I can see one of the other club girls walking over to us. "Away" is all I say to him. I watch the club girl grab onto his arm. "Come on, Buster. Let the little whore go" She tells him. He watches me walk out the door. Clearly, I meant nothing to him.

I walk down the driveway to the gates. The prospects at the gates look at me twice. "Open the fucking thing now" I yell at them. "Sorry, Kate. Pres ordered not to open the gate to anyone" one of them says to me. "Fine, I'll climb the fucking thing," I tell him. I throw my bag over the top and start climbing the wire fence. The boys looked at me like I had lost my mind.

I swing my leg over the top and start the climb down. I jump off when I am close enough to the ground, pick up my bag, wave goodbye to the boys and head off in the other direction to what I took a couple of months ago.

They don't care about me and wanna treat me like a child. Well, fuck them all. I am done. Buster can go fuck that slut who has been through most of the guys in that room. I am done. Yes, I am a victim, but today marks the start of my new life. I will protect myself. I don't need a club full of cunts to fight my battles.

If John or Brad come to get me again, I will fight them off myself. I am no longer Katherine Fowley, the victim. I am Katherine Fowley, the fighter.

I make it into the next town by sun up. I sit at the bus station waiting for the next bus to take me wherever the last stop is. I watch as one approaches from the distance. This bus is going to Castlemain. My apartment is there. I may as well go back to my home. I get on the bus and pay for my ticket. Taking a seat towards the back. I sit down with my duffle on the chair next to me and wait to take off.

Joel

She left again, and again I did nothing to fucking stop her. Even after everything, I was a weak bitch. Stacy still had her claws in my arm. I used my free hand to pull her hand off of me. "Don't you dare ever touch me again and don't you dare call Kate a whore" I spit out at her through clenched teeth. "You were the one flirting with me Buster. Not the other way around" Stacy says to me.

"Let's get one thing straight, Stacy. Kate is my old lady, and I have now lost her because of you and your whore-ish ways. Stay the fuck away from me" I yell at her pushing her from me. She stumbles and falls on her arse. "Fuck you, Buster. Kate doesn't want you. She has fucked everything that walks in this place" Stacy screams out. I open my mouth to say something when out of the corner of my eye, I see Diana making her way over to us.

The slap can be heard over the music in this place. "You speak about my daughter like that again, and you will never open your mouth for speaking or sucking cock again. You got me?" Diana screams at her. Stacy stands up to her full height. "If Kate were my daughter, I would have drowned her at birth" Stacy spits out.

I hear the gunshot and the thud of Stacy's body hitting the floor. "Fuck that felt amazing," Butch says from where he was standing. His gun still smoking from the shot he fired. "Anyone else wanna talk smack about my daughter?" he questions the room. A unanimous "No Pres" can be heard from all the members of the club.

A prospect comes running through the doors. "Pres just wanna let you know; Kate took off again. She went right. Shady is following her on foot" he tells Butch. Butch nods his head in acknowledgement. "Thanks, Frosty. Head back to the gate" Butch tells him. The prospect turns around and runs back out the door.

"What are we gonna do this time?" Diana questions her husband. "Let her go" Raider speaks up. "Shut the fuck up cunt" I yell out to him. Raider stands and pulls his gun out on me. "Wanna say that again?" he asks me. Butch raises his gun and points it in Raider's direction. "Lower your weapon, Raider. Or I will shoot you myself. You have an issue with Katherine, and I, for one, would really love to know what the fuck it is?" Butch tells his VP.

Raider drops his gun and puts it back into the holster. "Your daughter is a whore. Everything that happens to her, she brings on herself" Raider says. Never taking his eyes off Butch. "So, her being taken as a baby, she brought on herself?" Butch questions him. "Well, you and Diana did by killing Jane" Raider spits out.

All the men in the room run to Butch to hold him back. "Why the fuck would I kill my own sister-in-law, huh?" Butch yells out. Raider shrugs his shoulders. "Probably the same reason, your first love walked away from you. They knew too much. Wouldn't be surprised if you killed Wendy, too" Raider spits out. This man has a fucking death wish.

I make my way over to Butch and put my hand on his shoulder, whispering into his ear, "he knows something about Jane's murder. Don't get rid of him yet. Let me contact Bones and get him to send over Cracker". Cracker is Bones' charters torture specialist. He loves the thrill of breaking bones and cutting limbs off to get people to talk.

Butch nods his head at me, taking a seat in the chair closest to him. Raider walks out of the common room into the yard. Savage follows behind him at a distance. Everyone goes back to what they were doing. A couple of the prospects come in and clean up Stacy's body, wrapping her in a tarp and taking her out the back door, to the fire pit.

Half an hour later, Savage walks back in with a black eye and a broken nose. "Pres, we have a problem," he says then hits the ground, unconscious.

Chapter 13- Raider's past start to surface.

J oel

As soon as Savage hit the ground, everyone was up on their feet moving around. Men were running around the building. In and out of doors. Doc had come up to check on Savage. I helped get him into the infirmary. "He's been knocked out. I have given him the meds to keep him asleep. His body and face need to heal" Doc tells Butch. "Did anyone see what happened?" Doc asks.

"A couple of the men are watching the security footage now. Hopefully, it was caught on film" I speak up. Butch is still too pissed to speak. "When I find out who did this, they better say their last prayers cause, I swear to fucking god, they are dead" Butch spits out. We all nod our heads with him.

A knock on the door brings us out of our heads. "Pres, this footage isn't good, and I don't know if we should show you" comes the voices of Skulls. "I'll watch it," I tell Butch. He nods his head, and I leave the room, following Skulls to the surveillance room. He presses play on the computer, and I sit there waiting to see what happened.

Raider comes onto the screen, his phone up to his ear. I can tell he is talking but can't hear what he is saying. "Is there volume on this?" I ask Skulls. He passes me headphones, and I slip them over my ears. "Brad, it's Raider. Is John there?" Raider's voice comes out loud and clear. "John just wanna let you know Katherine took off again. No idea where she went this time. Find her and find her fast. My arse is going to be next on Butch's hit list" Raider speaks down the phone.

I curl my fists into balls. I stand up abruptly. I didn't need to see any more to know who attacked Savage. I march out of the room into the common room. I look around and see Raider sitting in the corner with one of the girls on his lap. I march up to them and push the woman off his lap. He eyes me off with a snarl. I pick him up by his neck and throw him against the wall.

"You're working for John" I scream in his face. His face pales at my accusation. He tries to deny it to me. "I just watched the video of you speaking to John. Telling him to go and get Katherine. Are you fucking kidding me?" I yell in his face. My fist flies up and smashes into the side of his head. The one punch knocks the fucker out cold.

"Put him in the basement. This fucker is going to die a slow and painful death" I yell out to the room. I practically sprint down to the infirmary to tell Butch of my findings, only to see him standing in the hallway door. The look on his face is one I have never seen before but is also one I never want coming after me. Diana runs up to Butch to try and calm him, but it doesn't work.

"Our VP is a dead man," he tells the room. All eyes were on Butch at this stage; they all knew he wasn't playing games. He follows the men down into the basement to watch over them and Raider.

Shady walks into the common room early the next morning. I look towards him as he approaches me. "She took the bus to North Castlemain," he tells me quietly. I nod my head at him, standing up and patting my pockets. Keys, phone and wallet in my pockets, I am ready to go. I walk over to Diana, who has her head resting on the bar.

"Di?" I call her name. She opens her eyes and looks up at me. "Katherine is on a bus to North Castlemain. I am about to ride off to follow her and bring her home. I promise I will bring her back" I tell her. She gives me a small smile and a nod of her head. Lowering her head back onto the bar, I straighten up and pat her shoulder gently. I turn and head on out the clubhouse doors to my bike.

I have been riding for the last four hours. My arse is numb, and my face is wind burnt. I have found the bus that Katherine is on, but I make sure to stay at a distance where she wouldn't notice me following. The bus pulls into a stop, and the driver gets off. Another driver gets on, but his face looks familiar. I get closer to the driver's side of the bus, and my blood boils.

I can hear Katherine screaming from the inside of the bus. I pull my gun out of my jeans and cock it. Running around the back of the bus, I see John pulling her off it by her hair. The other people on the bus are screaming at him to let her go. I get closer to them, his back to me. I use the butt of the gun and hit him over the head. He drops to the ground, and I grab Katherine and pull her into my arms.

"Go get your bag. You are coming back with me" I tell her. My voice laced with anger. She looks at me and scoffs. "Go back to your whore" she yells at me and turns to walk away. I grab her elbow and swing her back into my chest. "I don't have a whore, and the only woman I want has a death wish. Get your fucking bag and get it now" I tell her through gritted teeth. This woman is going to be the death of me.

Kate gets back on the bus but doesn't come back. The original driver gets back on and goes to shut the door. I stop him and step onto the bus. "Katherine Fowley, you would do well to listen to me for once in your fucking life. Get your shit and let's go" I yell at her. The bus driver stands up and starts pushing me towards the doors.

"This is my bus, and those are my passengers. No one gets off unless I tell them too" he spits at me. I turn so he can see my cut. His eyes widen, and he sits back down. "Katherine, you have come to the end of your trip. It'll be best if you get off now." He yells out from the driver's seat. Katherine scoffs while standing. "You have got to be fucking kidding me" she cries out.

I wait for her to get closer to me and wrap my arm around her waist. She tries to pull away from me, so I hold her tighter. "Don't fight me on this. The reason that fuck stain found you was because of Raider" I tell her. When we get off the bus, John's body is still splayed out on the ground. I kick him in the ribs on our way past him. I climb onto my bike and hold my hand out for Katherine.

She looks at my hand and rolls her eyes, throwing her leg over my bike, she climbs on behind me, wrapping her arms around my waist. I bring the bike to life and take off, back towards the clubhouse. Another four hours later, we are pulling up to the gates of the compound. Katherine is still holding me tight, so I can feel her body shaking with her sobs.

Pulling up in my spot, I switch the engine off and climb off the bike. Katherine tries to climb off herself, but I beat her to it. I pick her up and wrap her legs around my waist. Holding her under her arse, I head off for the clubhouse doors. "Why did you bring me back here?" she whispers into my ear. "Because they want you here, Katherine. You might not believe me, but here is where you belong." I tell her quietly.

The doors open and Butch comes stomping out. He takes one look at Katherine and me and blows a breath out of his nose. "Oh, thank Christ, you have her," he says to me. Katherine's body wracks with more sobs at her father's voice. I hold her tighter to me. I give him a small nod and continue into the clubhouse. All the men cheer at us. Especially for her. "They are cheering for you, baby girl" I whisper into her ear as I keep walking us towards the stairs. Tracy stands and stares at Katherine and me. I shake my head at her. She nods her head and sits back down.

Opening the door to her room, Diana is already sitting on the chair in the corner. I give her a small nod and take Katherine to the bed. I sit on the edge, leaving Katherine holding onto me like a koala. I kiss her head softly as she silently cries into my neck. I can sense that Diana wants to say something, so I shake my head at her. I mouth "leave it" to her. Diana leaves the bedroom and shuts the door softly.

I turn my body and lay Katherine and me down. Her sobs are starting to settle, and her breathing evens out. I watch her sleep and never remove my hands from her body. This woman is going to be the death of me. Just hope this time she stays put.

John

I wake up on the ground in the middle of nowhere. I know that I had Katherine again, but someone spoiled my plans. I get up off the ground, holding my head. I touch the back of my head and notice it was crusty. I pick at the crust and find that it had been bleeding.

I pull my phone out of my pocket and call Brad. "You need to come and get me from where you dropped me off," I tell him as soon as he answers. I sit down on a bench at the bus stop and wait for Brad to get here. I scroll through my phone and pull up Pete's number. I write out a message to him.

Pete, someone caught me again and took Katherine. I would say she is back in the compound with you. I need you to finish her off. I want it done ASAP. Send me photos for proof. J

Hopefully, he comes back with the goods. My phone starts ringing as soon as the text was sent. "Pete, why are you calling me?" I ask him. "Guess again little brother" Baxter's voice comes down the line. "What the fuck do you want?" I spit at him. "Trying to get my daughter again. Well, your plans with Pete are done for. He is now in my basement awaiting his punishment for fucking with the wrong people, and you are next little brother" Baxter tells me

I hang up on him. "FUCK, SHIT, FUCK" I yell out in the open. Fucking Pete getting caught has now fucked my plans up. Brad pulls up just as I am in the middle of my inner turmoil. "What's up your arse?" Brad asks me as he pulls up next to me. "They have caught Pete. My insider is gone" I tell him. "Don't worry about it. Pete was fucking shit as it was. I will get someone else in there. Maybe one of the skanks that hang around them" Brad responds.

I sit in the car thinking of ways to get someone on the inside who will do my dirty work when a voice in the back seat brings me back to reality. "One of the skanks was killed last night after running her mouth about Katherine. Are you sure you will be able to trust one of them?" the voice says. I turn in my seat and see Josh sitting in the backseat on his laptop. "What the fuck are you doing here?" I spit at him.

"Well, last time I checked I worked for you, John. So, here I am working" he retorts. "Another waste of fucking space, just like your fucking half-sister," I tell him. His face tells me he has no idea what I am talking about. "I don't have a half-sister. I don't even have a sister. What the fuck are you talking about?" he asks me.

"Oh, Josh, I have so much to tell you. Your Daddy didn't die in a war, and your Daddy is that fucking stupid cunt of a brother of mine. Just ask ya slut of a mother about him" I tell Josh. Josh's face tells me all I need to know. "Surprise kid. I am not just your boss. I am your fucking Uncle" I say to him, with a shit-eating smirk on my face.

I can hear Josh typing away on his laptop, probably trying to find anything to confirm what I have said to him. At least I know now that he will be on my team for life. He hates his father as much as I do, and by the end of this, he will hate his sister just as much.

Chapter 14- Surprise children

J osh

What the fuck is John on about. My father died in a war. He wasn't even around when I was born. "Brad stop the car" "Pal, don't be stupid" "I said stop the fucking car" I yell at Brad. He slows down and pulls over on the side of the road. I get out of the car, slamming the door behind me. Brad gets out after me. "What the fuck, man?" Brad asks me.

"Are you fucking serious right now, Brad?" I huff out a breath. "Your wonderful father in there just sprouted off shit about my life and you are acting like it means fucking nothing." My anger is starting to consume my thoughts. "He is lucky I don't unclip my whole magazine into his fucking head" I yell at Brad. Brad looks at me with anger in his eyes.

"That man was protecting you against the scum in this world. You should be fucking grateful that he kept you alive and not killed you because of who your father is" Brad spits at me. "Be grateful" I scoff. "I didn't even know who my father was until he opened his fucking mouth" I scream back at him. "Brad, just get back in your fucking car and fuck off" I yell at him.

Brad turns and walks back towards the car. "Think about what you do or say next, Josh, because I will not hesitate to put a bullet between your fucking eyes" Brad spits at me. He gets in the car and slams the door behind him, his tires screeching as he takes off. I stand still in my spot. Running my hands through my hair.

The only person I need to speak to right now is my mother. The woman who birthed me and then raised me to believe my father was dead. I pull out my phone from my pocket and dial her number. "Josh, are you ok, son?" she asks as soon as she answers. "No, mother. I am in the middle of nowhere, just finding out that my Dad isn't my Dad. Maybe you could explain this to me?" I say to her. I hear her huff on the other end.

"Where are you exactly? I will come and get you" She says to me. I send her my location and say bye to her, hanging up the phone. I find a bench to sit on, and I wait for her to arrive. I know this will be one hard conversation for the both of us, but it is needed. I need to know the truth. I need to see if I have been working against my biological father to hurt my baby sister.

A couple of hours pass, and I see my Mum's old beat-up Ford coming towards me. She slows down and comes to a complete stop next to me. I get into the car, and she smiles at me, but I don't smile back at her. Her smile drops instantly. "Where do you want me to start?" she asks me. "From the beginning mother. If that is who you really are?" I say back to her.

She takes a deep breath through her nose and lets it out of her mouth. "Twenty-seven years ago, I met a man named Baxter. He was this bulky, muscled, tattooed twenty-year-old man. He took my breath away. The day he asked me to be his girlfriend, I thought all my Christmases had come at once. He swept me off my feet" She says. I keep quiet to allow her to keep talking.

"He was in the biker gang by the time I met him. He was just about to take over from his father. He treated me like a queen. I never went without.

Being only eighteen myself. I didn't know much about life. Two years later, I found out I was pregnant with you. Your father didn't know. I knew then I didn't want to bring you up around that: all the fighting, all the sex and drugs and alcohol. I knew you needed better. So, I left. I packed my stuff and left while he was out on a run." I watch as a tear falls down her cheek. "I got as far as Old Town before John approached me. He was angry with his brother. Not allowing him in the club. Baxter knew that John wasn't strong enough to fight like him. He didn't have the balls to do anything of the sort" she sniffles.

"I didn't know what to do by the sixth month of pregnancy. I had started showing. Keeping it a secret any longer would have been harder. John made himself known again. He only had to take one look at me to see why I ran. He came to me one day and pretty much laid it all out on the table. He told me that if I didn't keep you a secret, he would kill you and hurt me, and I couldn't let that happen. You were the only thing I had left in my life at this stage" Her sobs are starting to get louder.

"John told me he wouldn't hurt me if I raised you as a single parent. I had to follow his rules and wasn't allowed contact with the outside world. All I know now is I will most like die by his hands. I am so sorry I never told you this before, Josh. You have to believe me that if I had my way, you would have known about your father and not the lie I told you for the past twenty-four years." She tells me.

I can see this is troubling her, so the only thing I know to do is hold her hand. "Mum, I forgive you, but it is time to face Butch. He needs to know the truth, and hopefully, we can work beside him to make sure that John doesn't hurt another person. You know John is hell-bent on killing Butch's daughter?" I ask her. She shakes her head no, with a shocked look on her face. "Is that who Katherine belongs to?" she asks me. I nod my head yes at her question.

She continues driving down the road heading towards Old Town. "Mum, turn the car around," I tell her. She quickly glances at me with her eyebrow raised. "If you want to live, you will do as I have said. Turn the car around" I tell her again. Mum slows down and chucks a 180, heading back the way we came. "What are you planning, Josh?" Mum asks me. "It's time to meet my father and for you to explain what the fuck happened," I tell her. Authority in my voice.

I see Mum shiver from the corner of my eye. I can tell she is nervous, especially when she knows Butch moved on. She stops at a motel on the side of the highway. "I need to sleep Josh," she tells me. I nod my head and get out of the car, heading into the reception to book a room.

Getting the key, I get Mum from the car and help her into the room. She lays on the bed and is asleep within minutes. I use this time to research anything I can about Butch and the Devils On Wheels MC. Article after article about these guys. All the good they do for the community. The kidnapping of their child made it to headlining news. What the actual fuck.

Mum sleeps for another few hours. I am too wired to sleep. My eyes are still scanning everything I need to know about Butch and Katherine. When Mum finally wakes from her sleep. We get packed up and hit the road. The drive to the compound is silent. I am too far gone in my head even to notice Mum is pulling up the long driveway.

My heart rate starts increasing the minute the prospects come into view. "Who are you and what business do you have being here?" one of the guys says to Mum through her opened window. "I need to see Baxter," she says to the boy. He gives her a strange look. "She meant Butch" I clarify for her. "Who are you?" the kid asks. "My name is Wendy. He will know who you are talking about as soon as you mention my name" she tells him. He turns and runs off towards the clubhouse.

He comes back a few minutes later, opening the gate wider for us to drive through. "Park your car in the lot and wait in it until you are asked to step out," the boy tells Mum. She does as she is told and drives the car into the lot. Sitting in the car with the engine off, I see movement from the corner of my eye.

The first person I see is an older version of John. "That must be Butch," I say to myself. Mum nods her head slowly. Butch approaches Mum's door and opens it for her. "Step out with your hands where I can see them," he says to her. She does as she is told. I am still sitting in the passenger seat, waiting for what is going to happen.

My door is being opened by the guy who is always on Katherine. "Get out. Hands where I can see them" he says to me. I do as I am told. He pats me down and removes my phone from my pocket. "Ah, your John's little lackey," Butch says to me. I slowly nod my head while taking a good look at him. I can see Katherine standing on the porch. Her arm is around her mother.

"It's been a while, Wendy," Butch says to Mum. She nods her head. "What are you doing here?" he asks her. Mum clamps her lips shut. "John" is all I say in return. "And who are you?" Butch asks me. "I'm Josh. I'm Wendy's son" I tell him. Butch looks at Mum and then back at me. "Looks like we need to have a private conversation, don't we?" he says to us, turning around and heading back towards the clubhouse.

All the men and women move to make room for us to walk through. Katherine's eyes never leave me. She knows exactly who I am, but I have never touched her. I was just apart of that shit. Mum and I follow Butch into the building and to a room off to the side. The table in here is as big as my apartment. Must be their chapel.

I watch as Butch takes a seat at the head of the table. To his right is his wife, and next to her is Katherine. Mum and I sit at the other end of the table.

Didn't want to be too close for him to hurt Mum or me. "Speak," Butch says. Mum takes a deep, shuddering breath.

"Baxter, I...." she says. "The name is Butch" he cuts her off. "Sorry, Butch. We have come here today because there are a few things you need to know. Twenty-five years ago, I ran. I ran because I was pregnant" Mum tells him. His wife and Katherine gasp at this revelation. "I knew I didn't want my child to brought up around everything you did, do. So I took off to make a life for myself. I needed to raise my child away from all the fighting, sex and drugs" Mum tells him. I look at his face to see it is still stony. No emotions at all.

"I was doing good until I was six months pregnant. That is when your brother found me. He threatened to kill the baby and me and drop us on your doorstep. This was just after the news Jane had died. John had a vendetta against you. He wanted you to hurt like he was. He threatened me that if I didn't do as he said he was going to bring the baby to you, dead or alive" I watch as a tear falls down Mum's cheek.

"John, he got his claws into Josh here and raised him to hate you. Think you were the enemy. He made up a bullshit story that I have had to stick to for the past 24 years. That Josh's father died in a war. John groomed Josh, from the moment he could walk. I never wanted it to be this way, but I had no choice in the matter" she tells him.

"You always have a fucking choice. So, tell me, Wendy, what the fuck are you doing here?" Butch asks her. "Butch, meet your son Josh," she tells him. Conviction in her eyes. The gasps can be heard all around the room. "He is mine?" Butch asks. Mum nods her head. "So, you mean to tell me that I have had a son out in this world for the past twenty-four years. This son of mine is then also working with his Uncle to kill his sister" Butch says. I watch the reactions on his wife's and daughter's faces. Katherine looks like she is about to pass out. His wife looks as if she wants to jump the table and kill us.

Butch stands from his chair and walks out the room, slamming the doors behind him. I turn in my chair to look at Mum. Her eyes are down on the table. She knows she has fucked up. I grab her hand in mine and whisper into her ear, "You've done the right thing". She shakes her head at me, "I completely fucked everything up, Josh" she tells me.

We are sitting in the room for 30 minutes before Butch comes flying through the doors. "It's the fucking truth" he yells out.

Chapter 15- Long, lost sons.

- -

B utch

    After I leave the room, storming out, like a man on a mission. I head straight to the basement to talk to my trusty VP. "Oh, Raider. I have a question to ask you?" I say to him as I reach his cell. "What?" he spits at me. "You're all buddy, buddy with my little bro. Tell me, did he ever let slip who Josh was?" I ask him. I watch as his already pale face becomes even paler. "You know?" he asks me.

Just the look on his face is all I need for confirmation—that boy sitting in my chapel. The one who helped hold my daughter hostage for things that were not her fault; Is my son. My own flesh and blood. I should kill his mother for hiding him from me. I should also kill my cunt of a brother for just being a cunt. I run back up to the chapel and burst through the doors.

"It's the fucking truth" I yell out. Diana and Katherine look at me. I watch the tears fall out of both my girl's eyes. Katherine stands and walks towards Josh and Wendy. The slap she leaves on Josh's face will bruise his cheeks. He allows it to happen. "You are a fucking cunt. I hope Butch hangs you by your fucking ankles and guts you like a fucking fish" she yells at him. Katherine storms out of the room. I can hear another door slam shut not long after she leaves.

I walk to Diana and grab her hand in mine. "I should kill you, Wendy, for your part in this, but take this as a warning. If you run back to John and tell him anything, I will gut you like a fucking fish and leave you to rot in the desert" she nods her head at my words. "And you, son. If I find you talking smack and trying to hurt my fucking daughter for that cunt of a brother of mine, I will gut you and leave you on his fucking doorstep. You hear me?" I say to him. Josh stands to his full height. "You have my word," he says to me.

I take Diana by the hand and pull her out of the room. Taking the stairs to the bedrooms. I knock on Katherine's door. "FUCK OFF" she screams out. I open the door to her room, "That's no way to speak to your father" I tell her. She looks at me and then buries her head in her pillows. "Dad, he was there when they fucking hurt me. Every fucking time" she cries out.

I go and sit on her bed. "Did he ever touch you?" I ask her. I know this conversation is hard, but it needs to be had. "No" she sniffles. I rub her back. "He never touched you?" I ask again, just to make sure I heard her correctly the first time. Katherine rolls over and looks at me. "No, he never touched me. He was always there when they did assault me, though. He watched me being raped and beaten" Katherine says to Diana and me.

I pull Katherine into my arms and hold her to my chest. "I will find out what the fuck happened. That boy isn't just going to be welcomed into my home with open arms. He fucked with the wrong family" I say with anger lacing my voice. "Butch, he didn't know the truth" Diana speaks. "Yeah, and neither did Katherine. You don't see her trying to harm her own family for a crime we didn't commit" I tell her.

Katherine's sobs get louder. I block her ears and scream at the top of my voice, "BUSTER". I hear footsteps stomping up the stairs. "Yes, Pres?" he asks me. I nod my head down to my girl, and he knows straight away. Buster comes in and takes Katherine from my arms. I place a small kiss on her head. "I promise to get to the bottom of this sweetheart. You will never be hurt again," I tell her.

Grabbing Diana's hand, we leave Katherine and Buster to themselves. I drag Diana back down the stairs to the chapel where Wendy and Josh are still sitting. I do not trust them, they have not given me a reason to trust them, but I will get all the answers I need from them.

"Wendy, what do you want in return for coming here? Is it protection? If it is that, you will not be granted. You tore my heart out when you ran. Thank god for Diana here. She built me back up from the shell of a man I became" I look Wendy in the eye and speak to her. I watch as she swallows nervously. "I never came for protection, Butch. I came because your son needs you" she says.

"I don't have a son. Especially someone who helps torture his fucking sister" I yell at her. "I didn't know she was my sister until two fucking days ago. If I had known sooner, I would not have been apart of it. Don't blame me for her fuck up" Josh yells. I look at him, disgust in my eyes. "I don't care little boy. You are not fit to be here in my presence" I speak to him, anger and disgust lacing my voice.

Diana grabs my hand and pulls me to her. "Butch, you need to calm down. I told you before; it wasn't his fault. He did not know anything. Wendy is the one to blame for all of this" She says to me, trying to calm me down. "Butch, I am not here because I want to be, okay. I am here because you deserve to know the fucking truth. I am sorry for running when I did. I am sorry for not listening and standing by your side; I had a child to think about. That child was my number one concern" Wendy yells at me.

"I also fell pregnant with a child, Wendy. But I didn't run away from all the shit. I stood by my man's side and never fucking left. What you did was a fucking cowards act. Thinking that you were better than everyone else. Well, guess what sweetheart? Not only did you fuck up Butch's life, but you had a fucking hand in raising a son who is a weak cunt" Diana speaks her mind.

I watch as anger flashes through Wendy's eyes. "I did not fuck anything up. I did what was best for my fucking child" Wendy yells at Diana. "You did what was best for your child" Diana scoffs. "What a great lot of good that was. His fucked up uncle got involved, and you thought it was fantastic to let it happen. You could have grown some fucking balls, Wendy, and came to Butch when it all started happening" Diana continues. "Butch would have looked after you and Josh, but instead you acted like you were all holy and better than everything else." Diana turns and walks out of the room, slamming the door behind her.

Wendy sits back down in her chair and puts her head in her hands. "I know I fucked up. I don't care what happens to me. I just care about Josh and his safety" she cries to me. I can't stand her fake tears. I have had many years of this shit to know when she is faking it. "Wendy, as I said, I will not protect you. You fucked this club when you walked out. Josh will need to earn a place here. I will talk to my boys to find out where he stands but right now. You are both nothing but enemy's of the club, and I will stand by my fucking words" I tell them, turning and around and following Diana's footsteps.

Josh

"I knew it was a mistake coming here" Mum cries out to me. "Mum, we needed to come here. Butch deserved the truth. Now I will go back to John, and I will spoil all his fucking plans. I promise you that at the end of the day, John will never hurt Katherine again. Even if I am the one to pull the fucking trigger myself" I tell her. I have made up my mind. John will die, and if it is not by the hands of Butch and the Devil's On Wheels, it'll be by my own.

We leave the clubhouse. I wrote a note for Butch to tell him my plans. I hope he will help me out when push comes to shove. I will protect my sister for the rest of my fucking life. I just hope Butch can get that from my note to him.

Getting in the car, I drive to let Mum rest. I know she has many mistakes to pay for, but I will not let my anger get in the way. Yes, she tried to do what was best for me, but she only made things worse at the end of the day. We drove for what felt like hours. The motel we stayed at for the night comes into sight. I pull in and book us a room. I need to rest and get back on John's right side.

I get Mum into the room and leave her there. Telling her, I just needed to walk around for a bit. I walk away from the motel and pull out my phone, calling the only person who will answer. "Josh, where the fuck are you?" comes Brad's voice. "At some shitty motel in the middle of nowhere. I am with Mum. I needed answers, and I got them" I tell him.

"John is fucking pissed at you. You better watch your back" Brad tells me. "What the fuck did I do? I needed answers, so I spoke to Mum. I haven't done anything that would make him pissed at me" I ask Brad. "He thinks you ran off to see Butch the bitch" Brad tells me. I scoff loudly down the phone. "Yeah, right. I would rather slit my fucking wrists than to see that cunt. He fucked with the wrong people. I have a way to get Katherine out of there and in John's hands" I say to Brad. My stomach turns at what I just said. I can feel the bile rise up in my throat.

"Good, hurry up and come back. You and I will get her and deliver her to John. He'll be happy with you then" Brad says to me. "Alright, I'll see you tomorrow," I tell him. After saying goodbye, we hang up, and I go back into the room to get some rest. Tomorrow is going to be a hard day. I need to act like I am apart of their crew and in it for the long run. I plan to get them caught; I want to see both John and Brad gutted like the pigs they fucking are.

Morning comes quickly, and Mum and I are back on the road. She is driving this time. "Where am I taking you?" she asks me. Just drop me off in Old Town. I'll find my own way around. I don't want you in the middle of this any more than you are" I tell her. She nods her head and does as I say. She drops me off in the middle of town. I kiss her on her cheek. "Get yourself out of here. Away from all of this, okay. I will call you when I have shit sorted" I tell her. She nods her head, and I get out of the car.

Walking down the main street of town, I go through the plan in my head. 'Suck up to John. Get on his good side. Act like I am getting Katherine, but get them caught out. Save my sister from these sick fucks' I keep repeating the plan. A blacked out SUV pulls up next to me. The back window rolls down. "Get in fuck face" the voice of Brad comes. I get in next to him.

"So, what's the plan?" he asks me. "Katherine is on a tight leash. They will not let her out of their sights. I will somehow work my magic and get into the compound. I will get her out to you, and then we leave" I tell him. "Wow, you thought of this yourself. I'm proud of you" Brad says, wiping a fake tear from his eye. If only he knew what my actual plan would entail. Yeah. I'll get on the compound, but he will be the one who is taken. Not Katherine.

It is time for my plan to take effect.

Chapter 16

K ate

After having my melt down, Joel stayed with me. He has this aura around him that can help calm me down instantly. That is what I love about him. He is the only one I want around me when I get so worked up like I did. Slapping Josh's face, I felt like a million bucks. I still couldn't get over the fact he is my half-brother, and he was there to watch me being assaulted, all day every day.

I get out of my own head and roll over to face the man of my dreams. He looks so peaceful when he sleeps. I softly trace his lips with my finger. I wasn't quick enough moving my hand away when his lips open and he grabs my finger in his teeth. "If you wanted a bit all you had to was get on top, baby" he gruffs out. His voice was full of sleep.

I push him on his back and climb on top of him. Making sure my pussy is resting on his morning wood. I rub myself back and forth a few times. "Is this what you want?" I ask him, seduction in my voice. "Only one problem, Princess," he says. I look at him. "Too many clothes on," he says and rolls over. Our hands make quick work of our clothes, and I am laying under him. "You got a condom?" he asks me. "Top drawer but hurry up," I tell him.

Joel reaches over and opens the top drawer of my bedside table. He grabs out a condom, making quick work of the wrapper and rolling the rubber down his shaft. Without warning, Joel has entered in me. The moan coming from my mouth has him thrusting harder and faster. The only sounds in the room are our heavy breathing and moaning. I love it hard and fast, and he just knows how to make me cum within minutes.

My orgasm washes over my body, and I clench my thighs around his hips. Joel thrust a few more times before roaring out his own release. He kisses me all over my face and finally reaches my lips. "I love you, Kate" he whispers on my lips between kisses. My heart starts thumping in my chest at his words. "Oh thank fuck for that" I whisper back to him. He pulls his head back and looks at me. "I fucking love you too, Joel. I was just waiting for the feelings to be mutual before I told you" I tell him with a smile.

Joel smashes his lips to mine again. I can feel him getting harder. "Remove the condom, dickhead" I tell him. He sits back on his knees and removes the used rubber, tying if off, then throwing it on the floor. "I'll pick that up after our next round," he says with a wink. He leans over and grabs another from the top drawer, ripping the wrapper and sliding the new one down his stiff shaft.

I sit up in front of him, grabbing his shoulders and pushing him to the side. "What are you doing, baby?" he asks me. "I'm on top this time. Now lay back and enjoy the ride" I tell him. He lays on his back, and I climb over the top of him. Lining myself up, I slowly sink down on his cock. Joel's hands go straight to my breasts. Squeezing them and tweaking my nipples. I ride him like I have never ridden before.

Moaning and panting, getting closer and closer to the edge, Joel lifts his hips up, and I come down harder on him. My orgasm starts rolling through my body and making me feel like I'm flying. "FUCK" I scream out. Joel smirks at me and keeps thrusting from under me. I lean down and plant my hands on his chest to hold me up. Joel wraps his arm around my waist and rolls us over again. He thrusts into me more and more until he finishes.

We are a panting, sweating mess but the smiles couldn't be wiped from our faces. "I love you, Princess," he says to me. I lean my head up and kiss his lips. "I love you," I tell him. Joel rolls to lay beside me, removing the rubber and doing the same thing again, throwing it on the floor beside the bed. "I really should clean those up before your Dad walks in," Joel says with a laugh. I turn my body to the side. "Well, at least he knows he won't get any grandchildren from us yet. They are all swimming together in the rubber pool on the floor" I tell him with a smile. Joel kisses my nose. "Fuck, I really do fucking love you, Kate. You have made me feel things I have never felt before" Joel says, planting a kiss on my lips.

I lay in the arms of this man. He treats me better than I have been treated before. Even after walking away from him and being a cry baby, he still looks after me and looks at me like I am his whole world.

A few hours later, we are sitting in the common room, having something to eat. A new female member walks through the room as if she owns it. I keep my eye on her closely. She looks like someone I have seen before but cannot place her. She looks towards Joel and me and sends him a flirty wink. I ball my fists up on the table. No one winks at my man and gets away with it.

Joel places his hand on mine, "She's got nothing on you baby girl" he whispers into my ear, leaving goosebumps trailing down my body. His words make me smile. I watch as this woman walks over to our table. "Hi, I'm Tessa. And you are?" she looks at Joel and reaches her hand out for him to take. "I'm taken" is all he says to her and smacks her hand away. I smile in victory at his words. "Listen here, you little slut. That man will be mine by the end of the week, and you will be nothing. So why don't you run away?

He needs a real woman by his side, not some little whore" this bitch says to me.

I stand up from my seat with more force than needed. The chair goes flying back and hits the ground. This motion causes the clubhouse to go quiet. "Who fucking sent you, Teresa?" I scream at her. "Oh look, the little whore knows who I am," she says to me. "Don't worry little Katie. I will take good care of your man when you are dead. He won't even remember who you are" she yells out. I eye the gun in Joel's cut and reach for it.

Pulling it out and raising it towards her head, I take the safety off and cock it. "I don't know what the fuck you want Teresa, but I'll tell you now. You will not be getting your hands on my man. EVER." I scream at her. "You don't have the fucking guts to shoot me, Katherine. Why don't you put the gun down? You are a weak little bitch" Teresa says to me. With my finger on the trigger, I pull my finger back. The bullet flies out of the barrel of the gun and hits my target where it counts.

Teresa hits the floor, blood pouring out of her head. Joel quickly grabs the gun from my hands. "Fuck, babe. Didn't think you had it in you!" he says to me. He fixes up his gun and puts it back in his cut. Dad walks into the common room and sees Teresa lying, dead on the floor. "Who shot her?" he questions. Everyone's eyes turn toward me.

"I did," I tell Dad. He looks at me with a look I cannot decipher. "Why?" he asks. "Her name is Teresa. She works with John" I tell him. The shocked looks on everyone's faces tell me that they had no idea. "FUCK" Dad yells out. "Clean this fucking mess up. Katherine, my office now" he yells out while he turns and walks away.

Joel grabs my hand and looks at me. "You want me to come?" he asks. I shake my head no, kiss his lips and follow my Dad to his office. Time for me to be a big girl and no longer the shy and timid little fucking mouse. I am a survivor, a fighter, a strong independent woman, who can fight her own fucking battles. No more will I hide behind the men in this place. John can come after me all he wants. I will be ready to kick his fucking arse back to where he came from.

I walk into Dad's office and take a seat in front of his desk. "So, do you want to tell me what happened out there?" he asks. "Stupid bitch walked in like she owned the joint. I am not going to take threats laying down, Dad. I am going to start fighting back. I don't care who I hurt in the long run. I have been through enough to last ten fucking lifetimes. It is time for me to take back charge. I have learnt that from being here with you," I tell him.

The sparkle in Dad's eye lets me know he is happy with my response. "How did you know her?" he asks. "She and John were fucking for a few years before he started on me. She didn't like the fact that he went after me and started causing problems for him. She never fully left. I caught them a few times and then when he was finished with her, he'd come to do it to me" I tell him. No longer is my voice waiving when telling the stories—strong, independent woman.

Dad hummed his answer. "You can go," he tells me. I stand up from my chair, wink at him and take my leave. Leaving his office, Joel is standing at the door waiting for me. "So, Katherine. Where did you learn to shoot a gun?" he asks. "Tracy and I learnt together. She thought it would be smart of me to learn in case of emergencies" I tell him shrugging my shoulders.

Savage walks out from the medical wing. He recovered in leaps and bounds. "Heard you shot a bitch" he says in passing. "I certainly fucking did. Bitch had it coming" I tell him. He stops, turns and walks back to me. Savage picks me up and swings me around. "I'm proud you little munchkin," he tells me. I laugh at him and hit his shoulder. "Put me down, dickhead" I tell him. He puts me back on my feet and kisses my cheek. "Next, we'll teach you to ride a bike," he says with a wink.

Joel and I laugh at him. "Nah, Sav. I'm happy to ride bitch seat with him as my driver" I tell Savage, pointing my thumb to Joel. Savage winks and walks away. Joel spins me to face him. "Any more surprises hiding up your sleeves, Princess?" he asks me. I give him my best seductive smile and get out of his grip. "That's for me to know and for you to find out," I tell him. With a wink, I turn and walk away.

Chapter 17- Raider's truth part 1

$$K^{ate}$$

It's been ten months since I was reunited with Mum and Dad. Over the past six of those ten, nothing has been happening on the John front. It is like he went MIA. We are not complaining about that, but still, it is starting to worry me. I don't know when he will pop up again and where he is going to do it. I know I should live my life like I have no cares in the world, but the constant reminder of his name, coming out of the club members' mouths, has me on edge.

"Kate, where did you go to?" Mum asks me as she sits down next to me. "Huh?" I ask her. "I have been calling your name for the past 10 minutes. Where in your head, did you go?" she says. "No idea. Just off thinking shit," I tell her. "Mum?" I call her. "Yeah, Princess?" "Has Raider been killed yet?" I need to know if he is still breathing. Mum shakes her head no at me. "So, he is still breathing?" I ask her. She nods her head.

I wait until she has left the room before I make my move. I head towards the basement and quietly tiptoe down the stairs. I can hear voices coming from Raider and someone else. "You need to get me out of here. Please" I hear Raider say. "You know I can't go behind Butch's back," the guy says.

I continue to creep down the steps until I am around the corner from where Raider is tied to the chair. "Please, Commando. This is bullshit. I have done nothing wrong, except speak my mind about that stupid bitch of a kid. She has done nothing but cause trouble since the minute she walked in" Raider says to who I now know as Commando. "I can't Raider. I am not going against this club" he tells Raider.

"You're just as weak as the rest of them then" Raider spits out. "No, mate. I am just not stupid enough to get caught like you did. I won't let you out, but I will get rid of her. I have my orders from my boss, and I will go through with them" Commando says.

So, John has others on hand in this club. Well, John. Nicely played but your plans are fucked, and I will be the one to completely fuck you up. I keep moving into the basement, slowly and quietly. On the table to the left of me is a loaded 9mm. It is time to show these cunts what I am made of. I pull my phone out of my pocket and open up my voice recording app.

"Commando, it's nice to know that John is your boss" I yell out. "Fuck" I hear one of the men say. I walk around the corner and see Commando patting his pockets for his weapon. "You looking for this?" I ask him, holding the gun up in the air. "You would do well to give that to me little girl. Don't want you to get hurt, would we?" Commando spits out.

"You think I am going to be the one who gets hurt? Fuck that is hilarious, Commando" I say while laughing. "No, Commando. I heard what you said. I heard it all. You are working with John. You are going to help get rid of me and then act like nothing at all is wrong. But I don't get why you won't help Raider out. He does also work with your boss, right?" I question him.

"Fuck off Katherine. You are just a cheap slut and a dirty little hoe. No one wants you here. Your Mummy and Daddy are just holding onto you to get John, and once he is gone, they will get rid of you too" Raider spits out. I cock the gun and shoot Raider in the foot. He screams in pain. "Shut your pie hole, fucker. I am the one in control here" I yell at him.

"Now, Raider. I have some questions for you, and I want you to answer them truthfully otherwise I will shoot you again and again until I am satisfied" I say to Raider. In the corner of my eye, I see Commando moving towards me. I move my arm to face Commando. I point the gun down and shoot him in the leg. "Nice try, cunt" I yell at him. Footsteps can be heard above us.

"Speak now, Raider. Tell me everything" I say to Raider. He spits in my direction. "I've got nothing to say to you," he says back to me. "Well Raider, I have searched your room, high and low. To find out why you wanted rid of me so badly, and let me tell you what I found shocked me to the core. So you might wanna start talking before I talk for you" I tell him.

The colour drains from his face. "You didn't. You're bluffing" he says to me. "I killed...." "Shut the fuck up" Raider yells at me. Cutting me off from finishing what I was about to say. "Spill it" I yell at him. "Fuck. Fine. I killed Jane. I strung her up and gutted her, making sure I removed that devil spawn from her guts. I killed the prospect to make it look like this club did it. What do you fucking want from me?" he yells out.

"Nothing now. Have fun in hell, cunt" I say to him, turning around and walking back up the stairs. I open the door and look at all the faces standing in front of me. I throw my phone on the table after pressing stop on the voice recorder. "You might wanna listen to that?" I look at Savage and Dad. I put the gun down on the floor and walk up the stairs to my room.

I had just made it to my door when I heard my father scream bloody murder.

~~

Butch

"Fuck. Fine. I killed Jane. I strung her up and gutted her, making sure I removed that devil spawn from her guts. I killed the prospect to make it look like this club did it. What do you fucking want from me?" I listen to the voice of my VP. Screaming out what he has done. All these problems started because of him and his jealousy.

If Jane wanted him, she would have rejected John's advances and gone with Raider. She didn't want him cause she knew how much of a prick he was. "FUCKKKKKKKKKK" I scream out. I stand up and start marching towards the basement door. "STOP" Diana yells. I look at my wife in the eyes. "You are too worked up to go down there. How about you take a 5-minute breather. Go the fuck outside and cool the fuck down" she yells at me.

I storm out of the clubhouse and into the yard. My anger is flaring. My VP is the reason my brother wants to fucking kill my daughter. I need to send that fucking voice clip to him. Tell him he is chasing the wrong fucking person. The doors to the clubhouse swing open, and I watch Savage walk down the steps towards me.

"Commando is apart of John's crew," he tells me. I look him in the eyes. "You have got to be fucking kidding me?" I yell out. Savage just stands there looking at me. "So not only does my VP kill my sister-in-law but my new guy gets clawed in by my brother and is working against me. What the fuck did I do in my past life to get stuck with these cunts?" I question the world.

Savage comes closer to me and puts his arm on my shoulder. "No fucking idea Pres. But I am here to get rid of all the problems. Now your daughter has shot both of those fuckers, so if we are to finish them, we need to get onto it soon" Savage says, patting my shoulder. I nod my head and take a deep breath through my nose and let it out of my mouth.

"Alright, lead the way," I tell him.

~~

Diana

I watch my man leave the clubhouse in a huff. "Overgrown man child alert," I say to myself. I hear a chuckle and look towards where the sound came from. Buster is sitting on a chair laughing to himself. "Oh fuck off dickhead. Let's go pay a visit to the scum downstairs" I say to him.

Buster stands up and joins me heading into the basement. He holds his gun out to let the guys know we mean business. "Raider?" I call his name. "What the fuck do you want?" he spits out at me. "I just wanna know why? I need answers, and you better give them to me quickly before Butch comes down here" I say to him.

"What do you want me to say, Diana? I killed Jane because she chose John. She was meant to be mine. I was just waiting for her to become legal. I wasn't going to take a minor. That isn't who I am" he says to me. "But you thought it was ok for John to take a minor?" I question him. He shrugs his shoulders at me.

"I wasn't there when he did. It wasn't my business" he tells me. No emotion on his face. "Pete. Seriously? You allowed my daughter to get kidnapped, assaulted and raped all because you were a jealous prick?" I ask him. He just stares at me. I think he was just looking through me.

"You are just as mentally fucked up like John. Good luck wherever your soul ends up. You will need it" I say to him. I turn to look at Commando. "I trusted you. You broke my trust. I will end you myself" I say to him. The look of disgust is written on his face. "Just hurry up and do it slut" he yells at me.

I walk over to him, winding my arm back. Bringing it forward, I punch him in the nose. The cracking of bones letting me know, I hit my target where I wanted. "You are my own flesh and blood, Cody. My baby fucking brother. You are out to hurt your own fucking niece. That disgusts me. What the fuck did she ever do to you?" I yell at him.

He shrugs his shoulders. "Just her breathing was enough to enrage me. She doesn't deserve anything in life" he tells me. I walk back towards Buster and grab his gun out of his hands. "Say hi to our parents," I say to him and pull the trigger. Shooting my brother in the chest. He falls backwards and moves his hands to his chest.

"You actually shot me" he cries out. "You were out to hurt my baby. I will always choose her over you. You disgust me" I yell at him and press the heel of my boot into the bullet wound on his chest. I stay like that until the life has left his eyes. I take a step back and look around the room.

"Buster, I am going to shower. If Butch wants to know what happened, tell him the fucking truth" I say to him. Buster nods his head, and I take myself out of the basement, up the stairs into my room. I strip off my clothes and walk into my bathroom. Starting the shower, I take a quick look at myself in the mirror. I always promised myself that I would never take the life of someone unless they really deserved it. My brother knew my feelings about John, and he still went ahead and ruined everything.

I just hope God can forgive my sins. I did what any mother would do. Protect their own.

Chapter 18- Raider's truth, part 2.

This chapter has violence depicted. Please read at your own discretion!!!!!

Kate

The clubhouse is full of chaos this morning. The men are running around like headless chickens. I walk down the stairs, standing on the last step. All eyes turn to me. I freeze in my spot, not knowing why everyone is staring at me. In the corner of my eye, I see Dad approaching me. "You want to play with the big boys, Kate?" he asks me. I slowly turn my head towards him and raise my eyebrow.

"Kate, you went down into the basement, alone, with no one knowing where you were. What the fuck were you thinking?" Dad yells at me. "What the fuck was I thinking?" I scream back at him. "I went through Raider's fucking room, Dad. Did any of you fuck wanks think to do that?" I ask him. Dad stares at me. "No, I didn't think so. So luckily you have a brilliant daughter, who thinks to do these things. And wow, the shit I found" I tell him.

I can hear little chuckles from around the room at what I had said. I look around at every single member before speaking. "In Raider's room, I found his diary. I read his diary. You guys have been living with him for two fucking decades. The man who killed Jane, as you would have heard from my phone. I was kidnapped and tortured because of him, and not one of you fucks did a thing to find out who killed Jane" I yell to the room.

"It has taken me ten months to work out that I am not a victim, but I am a survivor. I am stronger than I ever have been before" I tell them. Dad moves to stand in front of me. "You wanna know a secret Princess?" he asks me softly. I look at him and nod my head, yes. "To show the club you are strong enough to be apart of us, we have a little initiation you must go through," he says to me. I stay in my spot, waiting for him to continue.

"You are already apart of this club by blood, and nothing can change that, but, to show us how strong you are, you have the option of taking a man's life," Dad says to me. I scoff at him. "I already took a stupid bitches life, what makes you think I can't take a mans?" I ask him. "You see, Katherine. We have a way of killing; you would call it our calling card. If you are strong, you will be able to gut him like a fucking fish. Do you think you could handle that?" Dad asks. "How about you go back upstairs and think about it?" he questions.

I turn on the stairs and head back to my room. My mind is a jumbled mess. Can I kill him like that? Would I be just as bad as John and Brad, if I do it? What would the rest of the club think of me? Questions are floating out but not the question I really need to ask myself. I enter my room and head straight into the bathroom. Stand with my palms flat on the sink, I take a couple of deep breaths and look up to meet my eyes in the mirror.

"Can I kill Raider for his part in all of the shit that has happened in my life?" I ask myself.

~~

Butch

I have sent Katherine back to her room to think about it. I am pretty confident she won't be able to do it, but I had to ask. No one here will think she is weak because of it. Not all my men can gut a man, and that is ok. I am not that sick and twisted to make someone do something so vulgar and have them ok with it.

"Are you sure?" I hear Buster say into his phone. "Alright, keep me updated," he says to the other person. I look at him and raise my eyebrow. "That was Bones. He has men watching out for John. John is on the move. He thinks Wendy is his target" Buster tells us. I nod my head and turn towards my office. Sticking two fingers in my mouth, I whistle to get the attention of the clubhouse.

"If the word is true and John gets his hands on Wendy, we'll have a dead body on our doorstep. No one and I mean no one is to go after John. Wendy made her bed, and now she has to lie in it" I announce to the room. "What about her kid?" One of the guys calls out. "Her kid is nothing to us. He is a waste of space. If he tries anything to hurt Katherine, we kill on sight" I tell them.

Turning around, I walk into my office, slamming the door behind me. So many different emotions are swirling through my mind. The main one I feel is the anger I have towards my so-called best friend. He killed Jane because of jealousy. He killed Jane to get back at my brother. He killed Jane. I sit down at my desk and place my head in my hands. My heart is breaking at just the thought of Jane, being strung up and gutted, and to now find out she was pregnant.

Raider has killed this family. He is the reason my daughter was kidnapped and tortured. He is the reason I lost twenty-one years with my Princess. He is the reason I am who I am today. I trusted him with everything in me. I confided in him about everything, but now that he is the cause of all my turmoil. He is the cause of all my family's heartache.

He is the reason.

My office door opens, and I hear footsteps come in, I don't look up to see who it is until I feel hands on my shoulders. I turn my head slightly to catch sight of my Queen's legs. I stretch my arm out behind her and pull her in close to me. Resting my head on her stomach, I let the flood gates open. Diana just holds me while I let it all out. All the built-up emotions I have had for so long, are pouring out of my eyes. All the shit I had to deal with in my life is finally catching up with me.

No words were spoken between Diana and me. She just let me do what I needed to do and then once I had regained my composure, she took a step back. A knock at the door brings us out of our stare down. "Come in" I grunt out. Blowing my nose in a tissue, I just picked up from the desk. The door opens slowly, and my Princess walks in.

"Let's do this shit and finish off that chapter," Kate says with fire in her eyes.

I walk into the basement to see Raider sitting in the chair he has been in for months. He looks up at me with defeat in his eyes. "It's time right?" he asks. I nod my head at him. "I just wanted to say sorry to you, Butch. I know my apology means shit now, but I am sorry for what I put you through" Raider says. "You're not sorry for your actions, Raider. You're only sorry cause you got caught. You have fucked this club and family over. It is time for your punishment" I tell him.

Savage and Buster come in and drag Raider from the chair. Up the stairs into the common room. All the members of the club stand there. Some with angry looks on their faces and others with pity. They have worked alongside this guy for years, and not one of us suspected he was the culprit. He was the reason everything in my life went to shit. Through the club-house doors and into the shed, Raider is being dragged. He doesn't make a sound. He knows it is time to meet his maker.

The boys lay him on the ground and attach the chains to his ankles. "Any final words Raider?" I ask him as the boys start raising him up. Katherine walks into the shed at this time, and Raider's eyes hook onto her. "See you in hell, Princess" he spits out at her. I can feel the fire rising through my veins at his words.

"Raider, you know we normally knock out our.... Victims. For better use of the word. But for your complete disrespect towards my daughter. You will be fully awake for all of it. You will feel the pain you have caused Diana, Katherine and myself" I tell him. "You can't do that, Butch" Raider screams out. "I can and I fucking will. You fucked with the wrong family. You are nothing to us. Enjoy the pain" I tell him. I look to Savage "Gag him. I don't want to hear his cries" I tell him. Savage nods and does as told.

I stand next to Kate and hand her the knife. "Are you sure about this?" I ask her. She nods her head and moves towards Raider. His eyes light up at the sight of Katherine, holding our boning knife. He starts thrashing around on the chain, trying to scream out at us. Katherine holds her ground and kicks Raider in the head. "Fucking hell man. Just take your punishment like a champ" she tells him. The kick wasn't hard enough to knock him out, just let him see stars for a minute.

She stands in front of Raider's body. I can see her hand shaking. "You don't have to Kate. None of us would think anything different of you if you don't" I tell her. "No, Dad. I need to do this. I need to show everyone I am not that shy and timid little girl anymore. This man might not have stolen my innocence, but he had a hand in it. I want to show him that I can, and I will, finish him" she tells us.

I watch as my daughter grabs hold of Raider's junk. She has determination in her eyes. She stabs the knife into Raider's pelvis and starts dragging the blade down towards his chin. His intestines are the first to fall out of him. Katherine has a look in her eyes that is scaring the fuck out of the rest of the boys and me.

Once the knife had reached Raider's chest, Katherine makes a quick swipe of the blade from his right ear to his left on his neck. Her clothes, shoes and face are covered in his blood. She turns to face the rest of the room. "Am I a full member now?" she asks with a sickening smirk on her face. She stabs the knife into Raider's dick and walks out of the shed. We all stand there with our mouths gaped open.

"Holy shit. That is my fucking woman" Buster breaks the silence. All of us start laughing. Some of the boys are bent over holding their stomachs. "Clean this shit up" I yell out. I walk out to find Diana hosing Katherine down. Watered down blood dripping from her face.

"She do you proud?" Diana asks. I nod my head in their direction. "She fucking scared the shit out of us," I tell her. Diana laughs, and Katherine smiles at me. "Welcome to the club, Katherine. You sick bitch" I say to her and laugh. Katherine blows me a kiss and smiles. "Do I get my own cut now?" she asks. I laugh at her and run towards her. Picking her up in my arms, I spin her around. "You have made me so fucking proud, Katherine" I whisper into her ear. She smiles at me and kisses my cheek.

"I'm going to have a shower," she tells us. "BUSTER" she yells. He pokes his head out from the shed. "Come shower with me," she tells him. He smiles and runs towards her, throwing her over his shoulder and runs into the clubhouse. Diana and I stare at each other. "You gonna come shower with me?" I ask her. "Thought you'd never ask" she answers.

Chapter 19- Wendy returns?

K ate

You know the old saying, 'when it rains, it pours'? Yeah, well guess what happened? Two months after Dad dropped Raider's body on John's doorstep with a little note telling him that the war is on. Wendy turned up in front of our gates. Her head had been cleanly sliced off her neck. The note attached to her body told us 'an eye for an eye'.

I could see Dad was cut up about Wendy's death, but he also knew she had it coming. She played games with people she shouldn't have played with, and she lost. Fair and square, she lost. The only problem I am having right now is the fact my heart hurts for Josh. To know that his boss killed his mother all because of who Josh's father is.

Other than that, nothing else has been happening. Everything with Joel has been going as good as it can. A new prospect joined the club. He tried to grope me one afternoon, and I broke his nose. He has never tried to touch me again. He does walk around the joint like he owns it and snarls at me every chance he gets. I have been keeping a close eye on him. I don't trust no fuckers.

"Katherine needs a road name" I hear Savage call out. "Nah, she's a bitch. She doesn't get a road name" this prospect calls out. Within a blink of an eye, Savage has him by his throat up against the wall. "You wanna say that again, cunt?" Savage screams at him. The kid looks like he is about to piss himself. "Sav let him go. It's time I had a little chat with our new friend" I tell Savage. He looks at me and then back at this kid. "Thank your fucking stars boy. She saved your arse tonight" he tells him.

The prospect stands up and moves towards the bar. I walk to the basement door and open it. "In there, NOW" I yell at him. He slowly moves towards the basement door. As soon as he has walked into the door, I push him down the stairs with my foot. I watch as he tumbles down the stairs and lays out flat on the basement floor.

I follow him down and pick him up by the scruff of his collar. "You have come into this club with a chip on your shoulder and an issue with me. So, tell me what the fuck have I ever done to you?" I ask him. This little cunt spits in my face. I push him back and wipe my face with the back of my hand. "Big mistake," I tell him.

Before he can even move, I have swung my fist out and connected with his cheek. He falls back to the ground. I jump on top of his body and keep laying fist after fist into him. My anger is taking control of my body until I am ripped back, and strong arms hold me back. "What the fuck is going on down here?" comes the gruff voice of my Dad.

The prospect stands up, spits out blood from his mouth towards me. "No idea, Pres. This club whore just started on me for no reason" he says about me. My blood is boiling at this point. Dad walks towards me and picks my face up with his hand. "What is your problem with him?" he asks me. The audacity of my father right now.

I break away from the arms that hold me. "Why does it fucking matter, father?" I question him. Turning my back on him, I run up the stairs and out of the clubhouse. That prick down there has a problem with me, and I would really like to know what the fuck it is, but clearly, I will not get it from him. I jump into my truck and jam my keys in the ignition. Turning the engine over. I floor it out of the lot towards the gates. Shady is standing at the gate with a confused look on his face. "Open the fucking gate Shady" I yell at him. He quickly opens the gate, and I floor it out of the compound.

I drive down the road with nowhere in particular in mind. Why the fuck does everything like this happen to me. Things start going well and then bam, some prick turns up causing issues for me. What the hell am I meant to do? I find the road that heads towards the cliffs and take it. Driving up the uneven path, I don't have a care in the world.

I park the truck, jumping out and walking to the edge. I sit down and dangle my legs over the edge. "Happy birthday to me," I say to myself while contemplating if I should jump or not. Lost in my head, I hear the rev of a bike. I turn my head to see who is pulling up next to my truck quickly.

A little blonde with red streaks through their hair comes in view. She takes her helmet off and smiles a megawatt smile towards me. "Thought I'd find you here. What ya doing?" she asks me. "Wondering if I should jump or not," I tell her shrugging my shoulders. "Oh, Kate, what the fuck happened to you?" she asks me.

I look at Tracy, shrugging my shoulders again. "They are all quick to question me but never question the other person. I am made to look like a crazy bitch, and the other person gets looked at like they are the victim. What the fuck did I do in my past to cause all of it?" I ask her. Tracy sits next to me and wraps her arm around my shoulders.

"Well, Princess. Tell me what happened with the prospect?" she asks. "Where do you want me to start?" I question her. "From the start," she says. We sit there for hours, just talking about everything that has happened since that prospect walked in the doors. "Then today, he runs his mouth, I go to find out what the fuck is his problem with me and I'm the one made to look like a bitch. It's not fair Trace. I'm sick of them treating me like the bad person" I tell her.

Tracy's arm wraps tighter around my shoulders. She pulls my head to rest on her shoulder. "You have done nothing wrong. After you stormed out, which by the way was fucking amazing. Your Dad demanded to know what the fuck was the prospect's problem. He wasn't able to hold in all of the issues he had with you. And guess where they all came from? Tracy asks.

Looking towards her eyes, she didn't need to say anything. "Are you fucking kidding me? Even after him finding out the fucking truth, he is still after me?" I scream out. Standing up from my spot, I start pacing. "I'll never be fucking safe. Those pricks can say all they want on how safe I am, but at the end of the day, I am fucking screwed" I speak out.

Tracy stands and just watches me in my breakdown. She slowly approaches me and grabs my hand. "Kate, you are safe when you are at the clubhouse," she says. "That's fucking bullshit, Tracy. What would have happened if everyone was out on a run and I was left alone with him. He was working for John. John wants me dead. That little cunt would have fucking killed me without hesitation" I yell at her.

I know I shouldn't be yelling at Tracy, but she is the only one here. I storm off to my truck getting in and slamming the door shut. I punch my steering wheel a couple of times before turning it on and getting the fuck out of here. I floor it, only stopping for gas, food and bathroom breaks. I live on caffeinated drinks to keep me awake.

I make it to Castlemain in under 36 hours. The drive would usually take two days. I pull up at my old apartment building to see it all looks the same. I get out of the truck and enter the building, going up to my level. The door has been taped off with police tape. I pull it down and enter the place. It still looks like it did a year ago.

I start picking up the shit that is on the floors and rearrange the furniture that has been upturned. Cleaning the place from top to bottom. My mind is racing so I know that sleep won't be coming anytime soon. No one knows I am here, and at this very point in time, I couldn't give a flying fuck. I just hope Tracy is smart enough to keep her fucking mouth shut.

I spent hours cleaning the apartment. It is now looking like it used to. My phone has been turned off since I left town and I do not intend on turning it back on. Sitting at the kitchen bench, my head in my hands. I feel myself doze off. A loud banging at the door startles me awake, and my head slips from my hands straight down onto the bench.

"Oh, for fuck sakes" I yell out. Getting up off the stool, I walk to the door, rubbing my now sore head. I look through the peephole and see the back of someone's head. "State your name and your business for being here?" I yell out through the closed door. My breath catches in my throat when the man turns around, and I am looking at Brad through the peephole.

"You know my name and what I want. So how about you open the door, and we can do this the easy way" he says with a sinister smirk on his face. "How about you go die in a hole and leave me the fuck alone," I tell him. "Oh, no, Katie. I am here on a mission, and you are the end game. I know you have let others fuck you and now it is my turn before John gets you again" Brad says.

I do a quick look around the apartment for something I can use as a weapon. I don't have anything at hand, as they have all been smashed in the break-in. I know I should ring someone to help me, but my stupid pride is standing in the way. Brad is getting impatient standing on the other side of the door. He is still bashing it with his fist.

"Come on, Katie. I don't have all day. The longer you make me wait to worse, your punishment will be. Remember I have told you before that if you didn't do as you were told, I was going to ram it up your arse, dry?" he yells out. Flashing lights can be seen from my windows. Thankfully no windows are facing the front of the building from inside the hallway.

"Oh, Bradley. The police are here. I am going to look forward to watching them drag you away in handcuffs" I yell out through the door. "FUCK" I hear Brad yell before he takes off through the halls into the emergency stairwell. I know for a fact the police are not here but anything to get him away from me for five minutes is enough to let me breathe again.

I just hope and pray that he doesn't come back tonight. I need to sleep, and then I will move again in the morning.

Chapter 20- Kate keeps running

K ate

I wake early the next morning and grab a few things from the apartment. I pack my truck in expert timing, and high tail it out of Castlemain. I do not need to be here any longer than necessary. I drive north. Flying down the highway, I notice a car following me in the rearview mirror. This car has been following me since I left Castlemain.

I take the next exit at speed and notice the car is still following me. The windows are dark, including the windscreen so I can't get a good look in at who is driving. I keep driving, thinking where the next Devil's On Wheels charter is. I know there is one around here somewhere. Just trying to find it, is going to be the challenge.

I try to recall the papers I have seen in Dad's office. I know there is Dad's charter, and Bones' is in Newton. Where the fuck is the third? The next sign I see is a small town. 'Welcome to Angelville' I say in my head. The car hasn't slowed down behind me and are gaining speed quickly. My brain is trying to work out if it is here the other charter is located.

"FUCK" I scream into the cab of my truck. I hit the steering wheel as I come up to a set of traffic lights. Looking to my right, I see motorbikes lining the street out the front of a bar. All I can do is hope and pray that these are the guys I'm looking for. I quickly turn my truck into the parking lot as soon as my light goes green. The other car follows my move.

I jump out of the truck and high tail it into the bar. I take a quick look at my surroundings. "Help me, please. Someone is following me" as soon as the words have left my lips the bar doors open and John walks in. "There you are, slut" he sneers at me. The bar room goes dead quiet. I run towards a table full of bikers.

"Help me, please. My name is Katherine Fowley. I am Butch's daughter, I yell. All the guys get to their feet and point their weapons at John. "This is not the end, whore. I will have you, and I will kill you. Maybe I'll leave you like I did Wendy" he says with an evil smirk. One of the bikers shoots the ground at John's feet, making John jump back in surprise.

"I don't think so. You will never get your grubby fingers on this girl" the biker yells out. Another one steps forward and stands closer to John. "I thought after the truth about Jane had come out, your sick and twisted games would be finished," the biker says with a shrug of his shoulders. John stands up straighter and stares in this guys eyes.

"Butch still needs to learn a lesson and what better way to teach him than to take his baby," he says spitting the word baby out. The biker who is in front of John pulls his shoulders back and stands chest to chest. "Listen here, little cousin. You are not a tough guy. You are a weak cunt who hides behind a mask. It is time for you to grow the fuck up, John. No wonder Butch never let you fucking join" the biker says. He pushes John's chest, and John stumbles back a little.

"Just remember Katherine. I will have you again you whore, and once I'm done with you, there will be nothing left" John says to me and walks out of the bar. My knees feel weak, and I lean back onto the bar to hold me up. I already know I am about to have a panic attack. Gunshots go off from the outside, and I know already that John has shot up my truck. Black spots dance across my vision, and all I can see is the bar room floor coming closer to my face.

I wake with a fright. Laying on the dirty floor. "Welcome back, Katherine," a man says to me. "You know your Daddy is pissed with you," he says with a chuckle. I grab my head, trying to control the thumping in my brain. The guy who spoke to me and another help me up off the floor onto a chair. "So, little Katherine. Can you tell us why you ran?" the main biker asked me.

I just kept my stare down at my lap. I am too embarrassed to talk. "Katherine, we can't help you unless you talk to us. So open your trap and tell us what the fuck happened?" he says to me. I can tell he means business. I open my mouth to speak, but all that comes out is a sob.

I cry for a few minutes, letting everything out. "I ran because no one gives a shit. My uncle kidnapped me, tortured me, raped me, ever since I was 16. Now he is sending out other guys to do the dirty work and as soon as I stand my ground..." I say with a hiccup. "I'm the bad guy and the one in the wrong," I tell them, wiping my snotty nose on my sleeve.

"You know that everyone there gives a shit. Why must you talk shit?" I hear in the room. No one looks at me and owns up saying anything. "If you haven't realised, Katherine. I am on the fucking phone." My Dad's voice is loud and clear. "Now why don't you tell me why the fuck you ran and why the fuck I am getting phone calls from Danger and his boys?" Dad demands.

"I ran because you don't give a fuck. You were happy to listen to that prospect over me. You accused me straight away like I was the one in the wrong. You always accuse me of shit that happens. Maybe I should just let

John take me. It'll make your life fucking easier" I shout at him through the phone. I can already tell my words angered my Dad, but I really couldn't care less.

The sound of him smashing shit comes down the line. "Do not, and I mean it, Katherine, do not ever give yourself up to him. I will get rid of him and his fucking goons before they even lay a fucking finger on you" Dad shouts. "Danger, get her out of that bar and into a safe house. I am leaving tonight and will be there by dinner tomorrow" Dad tells this Danger guy. Danger grunts his response and hangs up the phone.

Danger picks me up by my upper arm, dragging me out of the bar. I look towards my truck and notice that all tires are popped, and the body is damaged. Danger keeps pulling me towards a tattoo parlour. "You will stay here, up-stairs for the night. In the morning I will move you to the clubhouse" he tells me. "And what you think John has left. You are leaving me like a sitting fucking duck" I yell at him.

"Oh, no, quite the contrary. I am staying here with you. I am not someone you want to fuck with either Katherine. You are my cousin's kid, so I will protect you but let me get one thing straight. You piss me off, and I will lock you in a fucking cupboard" Danger says to me. "Just like your other cousin then. He liked locking me up in small rooms" I spit out—anger in my eyes.

"AHAHAHAHAHA. You are so fucking funny Katherine. The difference between John and me, I will not fucking touch you. I will just lock you up and leave you in there. He would touch you for his own pleasure" Danger says.

I actually for once in my life, do as I am told. I sit on the couch in the living room. Festering in my own anger, but I don't make a sound. I stay sitting there while Danger is making phone call after phone call. I don't pay him any attention. "You want something to eat?" he asks me. I shake my head, no. "Katherine, you need to fucking eat. I'll order some pizza."

"I'm not hungry" I finally speak to him. "I don't care if you are hungry or not. You will eat the fucking pizza when it gets here and not complain" Danger tells me. I sit further back on the couch. Bringing my knees to my chest. I rest my head on my knees and look out the window to the town below. All these fucking guys are the same.

They all demand respect and what they say goes. Well, guess what, fucker? I am my own fucking person, so if I say I am not hungry, I will not fucking eat. I will not be forced into doing anything I don't want to do.

"Where's the bathroom?" I ask Danger. He points down a hallway. "Second door on the left," he says. I follow his directions and end up in the bathroom. Closing and locking the door behind me, I take a quick look at what is in here. There is a shower and a bathtub, as well as the toilet and a sink. I turn the light off and go and lay in the bathtub. I try to make myself as comfortable as I can, then close my eyes.

I am woken by the bathroom door being forcefully kicked off its hinges. "What the fuck are you doing, Katherine?" Danger yells at me. "What the fuck does it look like. I was trying to fucking sleep. Now fuck off" I yell back at him. Danger marches over to me and lifts me out of the bathtub. I try to wiggle myself out of his hold, but his grip just gets tighter and tighter on me.

"We have fucking beds in this place for that" Danger yells at me. Opening a door and throwing me from his arms. I land on a bed, and he slams the door behind me. I lay on the bed, looking up at the ceiling. I need to get away from this lunatic, I keep saying to myself. I move towards the window and try to open it. I feel around the frame to see why it won't budge, only to find the window has been nailed shut.

"You have got to be fucking kidding me?" I yell out. Danger pushes the door open once again. "There is no way out of this place, Katherine, so if I were you, I would just lay the fuck down and go to sleep. Your father will be here tomorrow, and I'm pretty sure his punishment will be worse than what I would do" he says to me. I flip him off and turn my back on him.

"You really are an ungrateful cow, aren't you? I am putting my life, and my members lives on the line to protect you. You do not deserve protection with the way you are acting" Danger spits out at me. "Well let me fucking go then if I am not worth protecting" I yell back at him. "Let me go and then you and your fucking club will live to see another fucking day. All I do is bring trouble" I say to him.

"No, all you do is bring shit on yourself. If you had just stayed with your father, this" he points between him and me, "would not have happened. It would be best if you grew up, Princess, and you should do it sooner rather than later" Danger says and then walks out of the room, slamming the door behind him.

I drop to the floor, unsure of what to make of all of this. I screw everything up. I am a screw-up. Today is one of those days where I wish John had gone through with his fucking plan. I wouldn't have to be here anymore, and I wouldn't be a disappointment to my family.

Chapter 21- Butch puts his foot down

B utch

This shit with Katherine and her taking off needs to fucking stop. She is playing a dangerous game right now, and I don't how much more I can take. The more she runs, the closer she is to being taken by John. Does she not realise that everything I do, I am doing to keep her safe?

After the issue with the prospect, who mind you is bleeding out in the shed, I sent her friend after her. When Tracy came back without Katherine, I was ready to put a bullet in her head. "Butch are you fucking kidding me? She feels as if you don't give a fuck about her. She feels that everything she fucking does is looked down upon by you" the bitch yells at me.

Lucky for her, Savage was there to hold her back. "I would be very careful with your next words, little lady. I will not hesitate to put you in your place" I tell the little firecracker. "Look all I am saying, Butch, is Kate feels like no one has her back. She said it was like, whenever something happens with her in the middle, you jump down her throat first. She is tired of it all" she says to me.

I take a step back and think about her words. Yes, I have been harsh towards Katherine, but this is the way I show I care. She needs to be careful. Not everyone here wants to be her friend. "Butch, I am not saying this to cause problems, but Kate, she's been through enough shit to last a lifetime," Tracy says to me. Savage wraps her in his arms as the tears fall down her face.

"Did you know what the day was to her when she ran?" Tracy asks. I look at her and shake my head no. "Butch, what is Katherine's date of birth?" she asks. I look at the calendar on my phone. "OH FUCK" I yell out. "Are you fucking kidding me? I treated her like fucking shit on her fucking birthday" I scream.

I walk out of the clubhouse and into my killing shed. Loading my gun, I let rip the full round into this little cunts lifeless body. "ALL BECAUSE OF YOU I TREATED MY DAUGHTER LIKE SHIT ON HER BIRTH-DAY" I scream at him. I know he won't answer, but letting this fucking steam off is helping me out.

Storming back into the clubhouse, my mind is set. We need to find her, and we need to find her fast. "Alright boys, we need to find her. Everyone take a section of land between us, Bones and Danger. She shouldn't have gotten far. Do it quickly. John is still after her" I tell the boys. All of them start moving out with me, Buster and Savage still in the room.

"Tracy, before you leave, where is the only place she would go?" I ask her. "Most likely her apartment in Castlemain" she answers. "Fuck, that's a two-day drive," I say. "If you move now, and don't stop, you'll do it in less," she says. Nodding my head, I move out to my bike. Diana is already sitting on the back of it. I raise my eyebrow at her. "I'm coming whether you like it or not, Baxter. She is also my daughter who I neglected, okay" she says.

Getting on the bike and bringing it to life, we take off out of the compound. Buster is riding with me, and Savage is staying behind. I need to leave one good fighter in case John goes there. I rest my hand on Diana's thigh. We both feel the same for how we have treated Katherine. She is meant to be our world, but instead, we treat her as if she is nothing to us.

I pull over on the side of the road after riding for a good few hours. Diana goes off behind a bush to relieve her bladder. I stand there, trying to think of how long Katherine has been gone. No word from Bones' charter yet. I have them on the lookout for her truck. She has only been gone for not even 12 hours.

Diana and I decided to stop for some food. Bones still hasn't seen her truck come past him. They are also looking around the towns near them. Sitting in the small diner, Diana and I are in our own heads. I look at my wife and see a tear fall down her cheek. Leaning over the table, I wipe it away with my thumb. Our eyes lock, and I can see the pain in hers.

"Why do we keep doing this to her, Bax?" Diana asks. I have no answer, so I shrug my shoulders. "I wish I knew, baby. I wish I knew" I tell her honestly. We finish and pay for our meals and head out to the bike again. "Maybe we should stop for the night," Diana says. I have to agree with her. We are both so tired. Emotionally, physically, mentally. All this shit is starting to take a toll on us.

I find a motel a bit further down the road and get us a room for the night. As soon as our heads hit the pillows, the darkness consumes us.

I wake the next morning, well what I think is morning to my phone blaring right beside my head. "WHAT?" I scream down the line. "I ran because no one gives a shit. My uncle kidnapped me, tortured me, raped me, ever since I was 16. Now he is sending out other guys to do the dirty work, and as soon as I stand my ground, I'm the bad guy and the one in the wrong" I hear Katherine say with a hiccup.

"You know that everyone there gives a shit. Why must you talk shit?" I yell down the line to her. I don't hear her respond to me, so I know right away she has no clue who is talking. "If you haven't realised, Katherine. I am on the fucking phone." I say to her. "Now why don't you tell me why the fuck you ran and why the fuck I am getting phone calls from Danger and his boys?" I demand.

"I ran because you don't give a fuck. You were happy to listen to that prospect over me. You accused me straight away like I was the one in the wrong. You always accuse me of shit that happens. Maybe I should just let John take me. It'll make your life fucking easier" she shouts at me through the phone. Her words have me seeing red.

I pick up the bedside table lamp and throw it at the wall. "Do not, and I mean it, Katherine, do not ever give yourself up to him. I will get rid of him and his fucking goons before they even lay a fucking finger on you" I shout out through my anger. "Danger, get her out of that bar and into a safe house. I am leaving tonight and will be there by dinner tomorrow" I tell Danger. He grunts in response to me.

My outburst has caused Diana to wake. "What is going on?" she asks me. "Katherine is with Danger. She is in Angelville. We are now moving. Get up, piss, do whatever you need to do but we are moving out in 5 minutes" I tell Diana, pulling on my cut and boots. "We are going to get our daughter back, and she is going to learn respect," I say, storming out of the motel room.

I sit on the bike, waiting for Diana, making sure I let the boys know where Katherine is. Buster is riding up to Angelville now. He said he'd be there in around 5 hours. As soon as Diana came out of the room, the bike was revving, and she was climbing on. She had little to no time to get sorted before I was taking off. Diana hits my stomach, her way of telling me I am in trouble. I shake my head with a little smirk. I like her punishments.

We ride for hours. Six, in fact. Rolling up to the compound in Angelville, we are met at the gate by Danger. I jump off my bike and shake his hand. "You have a very selfish cow of a daughter, Bax. I wanted to slap her a few times last night" Danger says to me. I can feel the anger course through my veins, but I also know that he would never lay a hand on her.

"Tell me about it, Daz," I say to him. "She's inside. Hurry up; I want her gone like yesterday" Daz says to me. I smile at that. "Is Buster here?" I ask him. "Tall, buff, pretty looking boy?" Daz asks. "Yep, that's him," I say. "Yeah, he is in there. Bloody Angela is trying to sink her claws in. Katherine hasn't come out of the room I put her in this morning. Better move fast before Angela is on her fucking knees" Daz says with a laugh.

Walking into the clubhouse, I see Buster trying to push this Angela away. Diana sees her trying to get her claws into Buster and takes off for them. She grabs Angela's hair and brings her head back. "My son will not touch a dirty slut like you, so fuck off back to where you came from" my Queen yells. I adjust my pants at her dominance.

Noise can be heard coming from the stairs. "Get your filthy fucking hands off me cunt" I hear Katherine scream at someone. "That there people, is my fucking daughter," I say out loud. The room bursts into laughter. I shake my head as she comes into view on the stairs. Katherine freezes in her spot. Shock written on her face.

"Oh look the little whore from the bar is here," This Angela bird says. "You need some more protection, or are you gonna run away now?" she taunts my daughter. Diana moves silently towards Angela and pulls her hair again. "If I were you, I would keep your mouth shut and only open it when one of those boys want their dicks sucked. You are not worth the energy of anything else" Diana says to her, then pushes her forward, so she falls on her knees. "That's where you belong, so how about you fucking stay there" Diana screams at her.

Buster moves towards Katherine and traps her on the stairs. She can't go back up as one of Danger's men is behind her and she can't go down as Buster is there. I can't hear what he is saying to her, but I know it must not be good, as the bright light in her eyes has dulled. I watch as Katherine's bottom lip quivers. I know Buster is being a prick to her, but she needs a bit of tough love.

Buster grabs her wrist and drags her over to me. The tears are shining brightly in her eyes. She looks down at the ground when she is standing in front of me. "Katherine," I say her name and watch her shoulders shake. I grab her by her upper arms and pull her into my chest. "I'm sorry, Princess" I whisper into her hair. Her sobs are wracking through her body.

"Thanks, Danger," I say to my cousin. He nods his head. I break away from the hug but keep an arm around her body, walking her outside. When she notices that she would have to ride home with Buster, she freezes. "He doesn't want me anymore, so I don't really wanna ride with him," she says softly. I look at Buster with a confused look on my face. He shakes his head, letting me know that he'd talk about it later.

"Katherine, you have to ride with him. There is no one else to take you" I tell her. She shakes her head. "I'll call for a cab," she says and pulls her phone out of her pocket, turning the device on. "No, Katherine. You will be riding with Buster" I tell her, with a firm voice. She stamps her foot like a petulant child. "I will not ride with someone who has just told me they are sick of my shit and would be better off returning to their original club. I will call for a cab and meet you back at your compound" she says, walking towards the gates. "You said what?" I question Buster. He looks me straight in the eyes, "Yeah I said that, but at this very point in time, I love that fucking girl and all she does is run away. What the fuck am I meant to fucking do?" he asks me. "Not say shit like that to someone who is mentally unstable" I yell at him.

"Fuck, Butch. She needs a fucking wake up call. I can't keep running after her all the fucking time. She needs to grow up. She is 22 for Christ's sake" Buster yells at me. Katherine heard what he said as she had stopped in her tracks. She throws her middle finger over her shoulder and runs out of the compound. "FUCK" Buster yells.

He forgoes his bike and takes off after her. Diana and I stay back in the compound as Danger walks out, pissing himself laughing. "Fuck you guys have your hands full with that one" he comments. I roll my eyes at him. "Look, she needs tough love, Butch. Being gentle with her will only cause more issues. Buster was fucking right to say what he did" Danger says. I know what he is saying is the truth, but I still can't treat her like that.

She is my baby, after all.

Chapter 22- Kate and Buster

K ate

Fuck him, fuck them and fuck it all. If he thinks I am too childish for him, well fine then. Maybe I shouldn't be with him. Perhaps I should just fuck off into hiding. Where no fucker can find me. "FUCK THIS SHIT" I scream out into the world. I keep stomping like a child, but that is how I am feeling right now, so fuck it.

"KATE" I hear Joel calling my name. I ignore him and keep walking. I have no idea where I am going as the woods surround us. "KATHERINE, WILL YOU JUST FUCKING STOP" Joel screams out again. I flip him off over my shoulder and keep moving, further into the woods. Hopefully, a big scary grizzly bear comes out and mauls me to death. That'll fix everybody's issue with me.

I am forcefully thrown to the ground, with a heavy weight on my back. "For fuck sakes woman. I am trying to fucking talk to you" Joel yells at me. He rolls my body over so I am laying on my back. I can feel something wet trickle down my cheek. He looks alarmed and places his hand over my head. It stings a little at his contact. "I'm sorry, baby" he whispers to me.

"Get the fuck off me, Joel. You don't want me anymore. You made it quite clear back there, so let me the fuck go" I say to him through clenched teeth. "Nah, babe. I ain't going nowhere. You are stuck with me for life" he says with a smirk. I start thrashing around under him. "You keep moving like that Kate, and I will have to take you right here," he says with a wink.

I scoff and roll my eyes at him. "You made it quite clear you were sick of my shit and would be better back with Bones. So why don't you fuck off back there then? I don't need you. I will deal with my own shit, by myself" I yell at him. Joel just stares at my face with an unreadable expression. I hold my breath while waiting for his response.

I don't get words from him, but his lips on mine. It is an angry kiss. Joel bites my bottom lip, hard enough to draw blood. He doesn't give up his assault on my mouth. I kiss him back with as much anger as he is giving me. Joel slips his tongue into my mouth, and I bite down on it. He tries to pull back, but I don't let go. He pinches my hip hard enough for me to gasp and release his tongue from my teeth.

"Playing dirty now?" he questions me. I shrug my shoulders the best I could being pinned to the ground. "You drive me fucking crazy, Katherine" Joel growls out to me. "Feeling's mutual, cunt" I say back to him. Joel smashes his lips back on mine, and his hand has moved from my hip to the back of my head. He brings my head up to him. Leaning back on his knees, he sits me up and tears at my shirt I am wearing.

Placing my torn shirt back on the ground behind me, Joel unclasps my bra and throws it somewhere behind him. His lips take a hold of my nipple, lightly nibbling on it. The warm rush of my arousal soaks my undies. "Fuck" I whisper out. I move my hands to the inside of his cut and move it from his shoulders. Joel helps shrug it the rest of the way off.

I lay back down, unsnapping my jeans. I can't afford to go back to the compound with all my clothes torn up. Joel grabs my jeans and undies together and rips them down my legs. He makes quick work of his own jeans and boxers, spreading my legs with his own. He lines up his cock with my hole and without warning slams inside of me.

The pain and pleasure cancel each other out. He thrusts hard and deep into me, and I can't control my screaming moans. Joel doesn't slow down his assault on me, spurring more sounds from my throat. I can feel my orgasm wash over my body. The high I feel and then the let-down, he doesn't allow me time between orgasms as when I come down from one, he changes positions to make me reach my next.

"Fuck, Joel" I yell at him. He keeps thrusting away, roaring out his own release, and crashing down onto my body. "I fucking love you, Katherine. Don't for one second think I fucking don't" he whisper yells in my ear. My heart is racing in my chest. Joel just fucked me into submission to him. No matter what happens now, I will always submit to this fine specimen.

"Fuck you, Joel" I whisper at him, with a smirk on my face. He looks into my eyes, and a smile graces his lips. "I just did, but you are welcome to fuck me now," he says with a wink. We get up off the ground, finding my clothes as we move around. "What the fuck am I meant to do about a shirt now?" I ask him as I pick up the tattered pieces.

"Just walk around in ya bra. You have amazing tits" he tells me, blowing me a kiss. I finish buttoning up my jeans and start walking back towards the compound. Joel quickly catches up to me. He was pulling on my arm to stop me. "Here, put your hands up," he says. I do as I am told, and he puts his shirt on me. "Now you will smell like me, and all the boys will back the fuck off," he says, and I laugh at him.

Strolling into the compound, Danger looks at us. "You're a loud one, little miss," he says. My face brightens, and I shove my head into Joel's chest.

Danger laughs loud. "Don't worry. I have the girls screaming when I fuck them too" Danger says. "Now get the fuck off my compound" he yells at us. I climb onto the back of Joel's bike and wait for him to join me. "Hold on tight, baby. We will not be going slow" he says.

I hold onto his waist, and he takes off at speed—Mum and Dad right behind us. Joel wasn't lying when he said he wouldn't be going slow. I rest my head on Joel's back and watch the trees fly by us.

We have been sitting on the bike for hours. My legs and arse are numb as fuck. We stop at a dodgy looking motel for the night. Dad and Joel go in and get two rooms. When they come back out to Mum and me, I grab a set of keys from Joel, kissing him on the cheek. "Come on, Mum. Let's go to bed" I yell out to Mum, heading towards the room number that is written on the key tag.

"Get fucked, Kate. You owe me a blowy in the fucking shower" Joel yells out. I hear him groan out loud. I turn to see Dad shaking his hand out. "Fuck, you have a hard head, Buster" Dad yells at him. "Serves you right, old man," Joel says to Dad, running for his life after the words are out of his mouth. "Hurry up and open the door, Katherine" Joel yells at me. I get the door open, and he runs into the room, grabbing my wrist and pulling me in behind him.

Joel slams the door and locks it. "Your Dad is gonna kill me" Joel pants out. "Serves you right, dickhead" I say to him. Joel puts his head up and has a predatory glint in his eye. He starts moving towards me slowly. "You" he points at me. "Owe me," he says, trapping me in between the wall and him. "A blowy" he whispers out. I blow in his face and push his chest. "There's ya fucking blowy. Now fuck off" I yell at him.

Laying down in bed that night, Joel wraps his arm around me and is asleep as soon as his head hits the pillow. Me, on the other hand, I'm wide awake.

On the outside, I am trying to show them I am tough and can handle anything that comes at me, but I am slowly dying on the inside.

My mind is telling me to give up. It is telling me that I am nothing. I am worthless. I am a disappointment to everyone I come into contact with. My mind is telling me that Joel would be better off with a woman who will treat him like the king he is. It is telling me that Mum and Dad would be better off if I wasn't around and maybe they could look after Josh together.

Maybe everything that has been said about me is the truth. I can feel the tears fall down my cheeks silently. Why did they have to come for me? Why couldn't they just let me go? Life really has it out for me. They say life is what you make it, but I never asked to be like this. Maybe I am now, though. I just want to give up and get it over and done with. Enough is enough.

I climb out of bed after taking Joel's arm off me. I leave the room and sit on the ground leaning against the door. The moon is high in the sky, and the darkness around it makes me happy. Being in the dark is what scares me the most, but it also gives me comfort. I know all about darkness. I have witnessed it enough in my short 22 years on this earth.

I stay sitting on the ground, bringing my knees to my chest, resting my head on my knees, silently crying to myself. I hear a noise and turn my head to where the noise came from and see Mum coming to sit next to me. "What are you doing out here?" she asks me softly. "Just thinking," I tell her, not elaborating on my answer. "Kate, look at me," she says. I slowly turn my head to face her. "Tell me what is going on inside that head of yours?" she asks.

I take a deep breath. "You have to promise me that you will let me talk and get it all out," I say to her. "I promise" she whispers. "For the past six years, I have felt as if I don't belong. I feel like the odd one out. I know a lot of it has to do with what I have gone through, but another part of me is telling me that I don't belong anywhere." I tell her. She does as she promised and has kept her mouth shut.

"I feel that everyone around me would be better off if I weren't here. Life would be so much better for you all if we either just let John do what he wants, or I end my own life. I am done. I am tired of everything. I am a failure, a disappointment and a horrible person. Look at all the shit I have put you through in the year I have been around." I feel the tears falling down my cheeks.

"I honestly believe that once we get back to the clubhouse, I should say my goodbyes and take off. It'll make all your lives easier if I wasn't here causing all these issues." I finish my confession. I can tell Mum wants to say something to me, but she is also lost for words.

"Kate, I don't know what to say" she whispers. "I know exactly what to say and what you have said is bullshit, Katherine" Dad calls out. "You might feel all those things, I am not disregarding any of that, but you leaving will not make anybody's life easier, as you put it. It will make us all more worried and scared for you. Why didn't you come to us earlier?" Dad asks.

"How can I, Dad? Every time I open my mouth, I am shot down. Every time something happens in that clubhouse, I am the first to be questioned. How the fuck am I meant to talk to you, when every time you open your mouth to me, it is to tell me I am in the fucking wrong?" I whisper yell at him.

"No, Katherine, that is what you think it is. I am trying to protect you" Dad yells at me. "I don't want your fucking protection. I don't want anything from anyone. I can look after myself" I yell at him, getting up from the ground. "Do not make any rash decisions, Katherine. John is still after you" Dad says. I shrug my shoulders at him. "I'm done, Dad. I am done. I don't fucking care if he gets me and kills me. I AM DONE" I shout at him.

Turning away from my parents, I walk down the pathway from the motel room. I need to get away from it all. I love them, but they will never understand what I am going through—mentally scarred for the rest of my life.

I now wish, Tracy never saved me the night she found me.

Chapter 23- The complete breakdown.

K ate

After my little breakdown at the motel, Dad decided we should get back to the compound as soon as we could. The ride back was awkward. I didn't want to go back at all. Getting back, I wasn't in the mood to talk to anyone. I trudged up the stairs to my room, locking the door behind me.

I slide down the door and hit the floor. My body has had enough. Enough of running, enough of crying. Enough of trying to live. I have done things in the past year that I would never have dreamed of. I crawl to the bathroom. Standing up is just too much energy to use. I close the door behind me and lock that one also.

I open the under-sink cabinet and find the box of pain pills. "Maybe, they will really understand now, that I am done," I say to myself on a whisper. I pull out the foil trays and pop all the pills out. Putting a handful in my mouth at a time and swallowing. They are getting stuck in my throat, and I cough them back up. Just to try and swallow again.

I pull myself up on the sink and turn on the water. Sticking my mouth under the faucet and taking a mouthful of water to help the pills go down. I never kept track of how many I took, only realising that I took them all when the box was completely empty. I dropped to my knees on the tiles and laid my body down. I was hoping and praying that the pills will take over soon.

The room starts spinning, dark spots dancing across my vision. I can start to feel the effects of the pain pills taking over my body. Before I completely lose consciousness, I speak into the bathroom,

"I'm sorry, but this needed to be done."

~~

Joel

We get back to the clubhouse, and Katherine's whole attitude has changed. I have no idea what has happened between her and her parents, but I don't think it is good. Butch and Diana have been very quiet towards me, and honestly, I am shit scared of Butch to say anything.

Katherine stormed up the stairs to her room. I went to follow her, but Diana stopped me by putting her hand on my shoulder. "Come," she says to me. I follow her into Butch's office and already see Butch sitting at his desk. "Katherine is unstable. She wants to leave. Thinks we all will be better off without her around" Butch says. His tone of voice tells me nothing is wrong, but the emotions on his face tell me otherwise.

"So what do we do?" I ask him. He doesn't look at me. Butch shrugs his shoulders. "Help her" Diana speaks up. I can see the tears are already falling down her cheeks. "We have done nothing but accuse her of all this shit. You are the first to jump down her throat when something bad happens here." Diana says, mainly to Butch. "What the fuck am I meant to do. She picks fights with everyone here" Butch yells back at Diana.

"Maybe we should trust her fucking instincts" Diana yells back. I am unsure of what I should do. I start moving back towards the door. "Sit the fuck down, Buster" Butch yells at me, catching me trying to leave. I move towards the chairs at his desk and sit down like I am told to.

"Buster we need your help. You are the only one close enough to her to get it into her head that we are here for her" Butch tells me. "I'm not the only one. It would be best if you had Trace for that" I tell him honestly. "Get the fucking little redhead in here," Butch tells Diana. She runs out of the office to get Tracy.

"I don't know what to do Buster. She is my baby who I have only had in my life for a year, and I am ruining it all" Butch says. I can see the hurt and the self-disappointment in his face. This big, tough, scary motherfucker of a biker now looks like a scared and sad little child whose favourite toy broke.

Diana comes back into the room with Tracy in tow. Tracy takes the chair next to me, and Butch starts his speech again. I zone out and start thinking of that girl who was scared and broken when I met her. She has made a huge improvement in herself and has turned out to be a strong woman—one who I love more than life itself.

"So what do you think, Tracy? Do you think you could help us?" I hear Butch ask Tracy. She nods her head 'yes' and gets up. "Where is she now?" Tracy asks. "She went up to her room," I tell her. She nods her head again and heads towards the door. "Give me half an hour. I'll see what I can do" she tells us, opening the door and closing it after she had left.

Butch, Di and I sit in the room for another ten minutes. We can hear muffled screams coming from upstairs. Standing up from the chair, I make my way to the door opening it. "Kate open the damn fucking door" I can hear Tracy scream out. "Katherine. Open the door, please. I just want to talk to you" she screams out.

"BUSTER" Tracy screams for me. I go running up the stairs to Katherine's room. "She's locked the door," Tracy says to me. I gently push her out the way, stand back and kick the door as hard as I could. The bedroom door goes flying off its hinges. Once it had hit the floor, I walk in. Noticing Kate wasn't anywhere in the room. Tracy goes to the bathroom door and jiggles the handle.

Knocking on the bathroom door, Tracy starts talking through it. "Katie, babe. Can you open the door, please?" she asks gently. When she gets no response, Tracy starts yelling again. She looks at me with a look of concern. "Buster, I have a bad feeling about this?" she tells me. "Move out of the way," I tell Tracy. She moves back towards the bed, and I run into the door, using my hip and shoulder.

I hear the lock break, but the door doesn't budge. I try it again. There is a heavyweight holding the door in place. I push on the door with all my strength, and whatever was blocking the door is now sliding across the tiles.

The first thing I see on the floor is the open and empty box of pain pills. Knowing I only put that in there last week, my mind is already telling me what has happened. "Tracy, I need you to call for an ambulance, Katherine has overdosed on pain pills," I tell her in a calm voice. I look behind the bathroom door and there, curled up in a ball is Katherine.

I slide to my knees and feel for a pulse on her neck. Not being able to feel the beating of her heart, I lay my ear across her mouth and nose, I feel a tiny little puff of air come out of her nose. "She is still breathing, but barely" I yell out to Tracy, she replays what I have said to the paramedic on the phone. "Buster, roll her in the recovery position, we need to try and get those pills out of her system. They are on their way" Tracy tells me.

I look down at the face of my beauty. I can feel my tears falling down my cheeks. Opening her mouth, I try to stick my fingers down her throat to cause her to vomit. "Tracy, I can't get her to vomit. It's not working" I cry out. I try sticking my fingers down her throat again, but nothing happens.

I put my ear to her nose, and her breathing is getting worse. I press my ear to her chest to listen to her heartbeat. It's faint, and I am stressing the fuck out. I can feel my own heartbreaking at this moment. Kate has succeeded in killing herself. I don't know how to feel. My soul is crushed.

Just then two paramedics come rushing into the bathroom. They look at Katherine and then at me. "Sir, we need you to step back," the paramedic says to me. I step back, gripping my hair in my hands. My mind is racing. How long has she been up here? How long was she laying on the bathroom floor? Did I kill her because of yesterday? "FUCK-KKKKKKKKKKKKKKKKK" I scream out.

I watch as they shove needle after needle in Katherine. Injecting her with different types of medications. I just hope and pray that we have made it to her in time.

I watch the ambulance leave the compound with its lights flashing and sirens blaring. My whole body begins to shake, and my legs start feeling like jelly. I feel myself beginning to fall until someone's arms grab me. I turn my head and look straight into Savage's eyes. "Come on. I'll get ya to the hospital" he tells me. Helping me stand up, Savage walks me to his truck. Tracy is already in the driver's seat.

We climb in, and Tracy has already floored the gas pedal. We are flying down the road towards the hospital. I am in the backseat, trying to hold myself together. "Buster, you can fucking cry. I won't think you are any less male if you do" Savage says to me. I couldn't hold it together anymore, and I completely break.

"Why? Why did she do that?" I say to Savage and Tracy. "Buster, Katie has a lot of issues. She acts tough on the outside, but on the inside, she is dying.

I went to her head doctor appointments, and this is what I came to know. What the hell happened out on the road when she took off?" Tracy asks. We spent the rest of the ride to the hospital, me telling them what happened and them just listening.

Running into the hospital, I reach the woman on the reception desk. "Katherine Fowley," I say to her. "Are you family?" she asks. "I'm her partner" I answer. "I'm sorry, is there any immediate family available?" the woman asks me. I can feel my blood boiling at this woman. "I'm her father, and this is her mother. Anything that is needed to be said about my daughter can be said in front of her partner" Butch says as he comes up behind me.

"A doctor will be out to speak to you soon," The woman says and goes back to her work. Butch grabs my arm and pulls me away from the desk. "Don't start shit here?" he tells me, pulling me towards the chairs. We sit down and stay there, waiting for hours. A doctor comes out from the back, "Family of Katherine Fowley?" he asks. Butch, Di and I stand up. We move towards the doctor, and I can already feel my heartbreaking.

"Follow me, please," the doctor says. We start walking down a hallway. The letters ICU are written above a door. The doctor keeps us walking further down the hallway, opening a door at the end. He waves his hand for us to enter. Butch sits on a chair and pulls Di onto his lap to leave the other chair for me. "Please have a seat," the doc says to me. I shake my head at him. "Sit down, Buster," Butch says to me. I sit down at his demand.

"Katherine has overdosed on pain medication. She is in a coma. We have tried to get everything out of her system, but we don't know if she will recover. The next 24 to 48 hours are going to be the hardest. I'm sorry I couldn't offer you different news" the doc says. Diana sobs into Butch's shoulder. "What are the chances, Doc?" I ask him. He looks at me and shakes his head. "I can't give you guys a percentage. Katherine took a fair amount. I personally don't like the outlook on this. I am sorry I can't give you guys anything else" he says to us.

"Can we see her?" Butch asks. "Of course. Give me a moment, and I'll go and check to make sure she is ready for visitors" the doc says and leaves the room. I sit forward in my chair and rest my head in my hands. I watch as my tears fall from my cheeks to the carpet below. "This is all my fault. I am so sorry" I say to Butch and Di.

"Don't Buster. It isn't your fault. We didn't see the fucking signs. This is on us more than it is on you" Butch says to me. I shake my head at him. I was the one who said I would be better off going back to Bones. My mind is a mess. The door opens, and the doctor sticks his head in. "Come. You won't be able to stay long but follow me" he says. We get up and follow him back down the hallway towards ICU.

Entering in the room where Katherine is laying in the bed—attached to all different tubes and wires. My heart breaks at seeing her like this, not knowing if she will ever wake up again and if she does, what kind of memory will she have. Will she remember any of us? Butch and Diana give her a kiss on her head. Butch pats my shoulder and walks out with his arm wrapped around his wife.

I take Katherine's hand in mine and sit on the chair next to her bed. "I'm so sorry, Kate. I never meant to hurt you with my words, but now I know I did. Please come back to me, and I promise I will look after you until my dying breath. I love you" I tell her and kiss her knuckles. I place her hand back on the bed, get up and walk out of her room, taking one last glance of her over my shoulder.

Chapter 24- How much longer?

J oel

The past couple of weeks have been hard on every single member of the club. No one wanted to go out and do runs. No one wanted to open up the businesses. Butch had to force everyone to try and get back to normality, even though he was broken inside.

I would spend every waking moment at the hospital with Kate. I would hold her hand and talk to her like she was still there with me. "Please, beautiful. I need you to come back to me" I say to her. I tell her about the club and her parents. I talk about Tracy and Savage. He finally claimed her. Only took them nearly a year to get their shit together.

"Kate, please. Show me something" I would ask of her. But I would get nothing in return. Her heart rate was always steady, and a machine was doing her breathing. The doctors have said that she isn't brain dead, and that is why they are leaving her on the ventilator. I just wish she would open her eyes for me.

Two months have passed now. I am making my normal trip into the hospital to sit with Katherine. I learnt from the physiotherapist how to do exercises with her so her muscles wouldn't deteriorate. The sooner she wakes up, the sooner she will be back to her usual self. I have hope in her abilities.

Morning to night, I sit with Kate. I cry, I smile, and then I cry again. I need her with me. I need her by my side. I wish I had told her all of this. I wish....... I just wish she was here with me right now. The hospital room door opens, and I turn my neck to look at who is coming in. "How is she today?" the small voice of Diana asks. "No change," I tell her softly.

Diana walks over to me and places her hand on my shoulder. "She'll come back to us, Joel. She is a Fowley after all" she tells me. I just wish I could take her words and run with them. The pain in my heart from the way I treated Kate is killing me what I would give to be able to swap places with her.

Diana moves around to the other side of Kate's bed and holds her hand. "Hey, Princess. Can you please show us you are still with us? We all miss you at home." Diana says to her. I'm holding her other hand gently. Katherine's fingers tighten around my hand.

"Katherine, can you do that again?" I ask her, but get nothing in return. My heart rate had increased, but now it is breaking once again. "What happened?" Diana asks. "She squeezed my hand," I tell her. Diana looked hopeful, but that glint in her eye vanished when she saw my emotions surfacing again.

"She will come out of this. I just know it. You gotta have faith" Diana tells me. I give Di a small smile and stand up. "I really should get some work done before Butch fires me," I tell her with a little laugh. Di smiles at me and shakes her head. "You are the only fucker he will take it easy on. The rest of them, may God have mercy on their souls" she says and laughs out loud.

Leaving the hospital, I kick start my bike taking off with a cloud of dust behind me. I ride back to the clubhouse, with a feeling of dread the whole time. There is something not right as I pull up to the gates. There's a man standing on the path next to the driveway watching the clubhouse. I slow my bike down and look at him, trying to work out what he wants.

I get off my bike and slowly approach him. Keeping my hands at my sides, ready to grab my gun if needed. "Can I help you?" I ask him. He turns to look at me. His face is all beat up. Black and blue bruises from his eyes to his chin. "Are you Butch?" he asks me. I shake my head, no. "Do you know where I will find him?" he asks again.

I keep staring at him. "What do you want with Butch?" I ask. "I have a package for him," he tells me. "I can give it to him," I say to this guy. I'm not sure if he even knows what's going on. His eyes are spacy. He is swaying on his feet. "Mate, what the fuck happened to you?" I ask him. I watch as his eyes roll into the back of his head, and he hits the concrete underneath him.

Moving quickly over to him, I bend down and check for a pulse. I can't find one on his neck or wrists. "Holy shit" I yell out. One of the prospects hears me and comes running over. "Buster" he calls my name. "Frosty, get Butch out here," I tell him. Frosty runs off into the compound to get Butch. Two minutes later, Butch is standing next to me looking down at this guy.

"Roll him over," Butch says to me. I roll the guy over and notice the stab wounds in his back. "Fuck" Butch yells out. "John has done this," he says. Anger lacing his voice. Butch bends down and helps me pick the guy up off the ground. We take him into the compound and lay him on the front porch. "Check all his pockets," Butch tells me.

I stick my hand into the front of his jeans and pull out a USB drive. "There would have to be something on this. He did tell me he had a package for you before he went down" I tell Butch. Butch takes the USB from me and walks into the clubhouse. I finish checking this guys pockets and come up empty. All he had on him was the USB stick, and that was it.

I stand up and move into the clubhouse. On the main TV is a picture that makes my blood boil and vomit rise up my throat. On the screen is my Katherine. My Katherine, who is in a coma in the hospital. Someone has been in her room with her of a night. They have been filming her. Touching her. Making rude and lude comments to her.

I turn around and storm back out of the clubhouse. My bike is still sitting out the front of the compound. I walk straight through the gates and jump onto my bike. Starting it as quick as I can, I take off down the road towards the hospital. Not obeying speed signs, I get there as quick as I can.

I run into the main doors, "Sir, it is past visiting hours" a woman yells at me. "If it is past visiting hours, why the hell did my boss get a video of a man, in his daughter's hospital room, after visiting hours?" I ask her. She can't answer me. "My bosses daughter will be having round the clock protection. If you do not like it, find somewhere else to work" I tell her. Pressing the button for the elevator.

Finally, the elevator comes to a stop on Kate's floor. I walk through the doors and wait for others to open from the inside. I make it to her room and hear voices from the inside. I put my hand on my gun and slowly open the door. Two doctors are standing at the foot of her bed. "She has been in a coma for just over two months now. The poor girl tried to take her own life" the doctor on the left says to the other.

"I would too if I was stuck with those bikie scum out there," the other doctor says. His voice sounds familiar. I push the door wider and walk-in. "I'm sorry sir, visiting hours are over," the first doctor says. "I'm not leaving this

hospital. Katherine will have 24 hours a day seven days a week protection"
I tell him. He looks at me nervously.

I take a good look at the other doctor in the room. He won't look me in the
eye. I move in closer to him and can feel him tense up beside me. "I know
who you are. You are no doctor here" I whisper into his ear. He lets out a
rugged breath. I nod my head at the other doctor, telling him to leave the
room. He takes my cue and walks out. "Now, we are alone. What the fuck
are you doing here?" I ask him.

"Go fuck yourself." He says back to me. "Nah, I wouldn't mind taking you
for a bit. Just think of all the fun we can have. Especially when I go in dry"
I say to him and lick his ear lobe. He pales even more. "Please, John told
me to come here and act like a doctor and get into her room. I promise I
never touched her" he tries to reason with me.

"I saw the video. Did touching a barely alive woman make you feel all
manly?" I ask him, stepping back from his body. Grabbing my gun out of
my cut and applying the silencer. "Did you feel all big and tough, touching
and threatening a woman who is in a coma?" I continue to ask questions.
He never turns around to look me in the eyes.

"Tell me. Did you feel like a fucking man every time you came in here with
the video camera? Every time you touched her body? Every time you made
a disgusting comment towards her? ANSWER ME. DID YOU? I yell at
him. He shakes his head at my questions. "No, no, it was nothing like that.
I swear. I never even wanted to do it, but John said he'd kill my wife and
kids if I didn't" he cries out.

"I don't have any sympathy for pricks like you. You were there when John
assaulted this girl. Did you know she is blood to him? Might not be direct
parental blood, but that is his niece. His only fucking niece and he raped
her and tortured her, all for what? Revenge on his woman's death that no
one here committed" I yell at him.

"I don't care, you have a wife and kids. You made your bed, and now you are to sleep in it" I tell him without an ounce of care in the world. I raise my gun to his head and pull the trigger. I watch as the bullet enters into his skull and exits through the back of it. He drops to the floor, and the blood runs out onto the floor below him.

Pulling my phone out of my pocket, I dial the number to my Pres. "Buster" he answers. "Kate's room at the hospital had an accident. There is blood all over the floor. I don't know how it happened. Kate is unharmed though" I tell him. Butch grunts down the line. "See you in thirty," he says and hangs up.

There is going to be a bit of damage control done here, but that's ok. He wasn't even a real doctor. I lock the door to Katherine's room. I don't need any nurses coming in and seeing the dead body. Grabbing a sheet off the shelf in the corner, I cover the body. Guys like him, grind my fucking gears. Don't pull the wife and kids card on me. You are in the fucking wrong in the first place.

True to his word, Butch walks in the room not even half an hour later, two prospects in toe. "Clean this mess up and then stand guard at the door," Butch tells the prospects. They nod their heads and get to work. "Hopefully, shit will change now," he tells me.

~~

Two months later

Joel

Another two months have passed. Katherine has sent us on a crazy ride over the last couple of months. One minute she is crashing, the next her body is reacting to our voices. Doctors think she will wake up now. She is breathing on her own now, so that tube has been removed—one less thing to worry about.

John hasn't tried to send any more men in to watch Katherine. He knows he got caught the last time. I sort of feel sorry for that guy's family, but he fucked up by listening to John in the first place.

Sitting by Kate's bed, like I have done for the last seventeen weeks, just holding her hand. "Come on, baby. We all miss you at home" I tell her. Like I have told her for the past seventeen weeks. Her hand twitches again, but this time she holds on and doesn't let go.

"Kate, open your eyes, baby girl. Please open your eyes" I plead with her. Her eyelids flutter, but then everything stops. I sit back in my chair and look down at the floor. Letting the tears fall from my cheeks. Katherine squeezes my hand again. I don't get excited like I did the last time, knowing that she would just stop again.

Her hand keeps squeezing mine, and I gasp when I look up.

Chapter 25- She's awake

Butch

My phone keeps ringing, and I keep ignoring it. It starts and stops, starts and stops. I finally check it and see I have ten missed calls from Buster. Quickly dialling him back, "Butch, get yourself and Di to the hospital now," he says to me. "Why? What's wrong?" I ask him. "Nothing wrong, Butch, but Kate...... she's awake," he tells me. I can feel the tension in my body melting away. "I'll be there soon," I tell him and hang up the phone.

I run out of the office into the common room where all the men are. "SHE'S AWAKE" I yell out. The clubhouse comes alive with all the members cheering. Diana is sitting at a table in the corner, and I can see the tears of happiness falling from her eyes.

It has been four months since she tried to take her own life. Four months of constant heartache. Four months of not knowing what is going on. I walk over to Diana and grab her hands. "Let's go see our baby," I tell her. She stands up and wraps her arms around me. I wrap my own around her, and we hug for a while.

Wiping our tears off our faces, we head out to the bike. Jumping and on and starting it, we are quickly on the road towards the hospital to see our girl. No issues following us around and we make it there in twenty minutes. I park the bike, and we both climb off, racing into the main doors to the elevator, taking it up to Katherine's floor.

I'm dragging Diana behind me as we rush through the hallways making our way to her room. The door is open to Katherine's room. We walk in and see her sitting there looking at Buster. No words are being spoken. She turns her head and looks towards Diana and me. I smile at her, and she turns her head away.

"Kate, please. We are all here for you. Why won't you talk to us?" Buster asks her. Kate keeps her head facing the other way. It was like she doesn't want us there with her. "Katherine" Diana calls. Katherine doesn't even look at her mother, she just points towards the door. She was telling us to leave her alone.

Diana lets out a heart-shattering sob and runs from the room. I take after her, catching up with her in the hallway. Pulling her back towards me and just holding her as tight as I can. "She will come around. We did this for her" I tell Diana, kissing the top of her head.

"GET THE FUCK OUT OF MY ROOM" we hear Katherine scream. Buster walks out, slamming the door behind him. I can see the pain on his face. He doesn't see us standing down the hallway. I watch Buster slide down the wall and put his head in his hands. I walk over to him and sit next to him on the floor. "She will come around," I tell Buster, just like I told Diana, not too long ago.

His shoulders start shaking. I have no idea how to comfort a man crying, so I look to Di, to help me out. She comes over and squats down in front of Buster. She grabs his hands, and he lifts his head up. She gives him a look, and he knows straight away. I watch as my wife and my daughter's boyfriend hold each other and cry.

I stand up and look in through the window at Katherine. She is still looking away from us. I just wish I knew what was going through her head. A doctor walks past us, and I stop him. "Doc, what is going on with my daughter? Why has she woken up in a bitchy mood?" I ask him. He just looks at me. "Sir, your daughter has just woken up from a four-month coma. She tried to take her own life for reasons unknown. Give your daughter a break" the doctor says and walks away. I'm shocked at the way he just spoke to me. He is lucky we are in a fucking hospital.

I go back to looking into Kate's room. We make eye contact. I watch her as she watches me. I point into her room, and she slowly nods her head. I walk in slowly, closing the door behind me. "What do you want?" she asks me. "Kate, we have all been worried about you," I tell her. She scoffs at me.

I pull up a chair next to her bedside and sit down. I need to choose my words carefully here. "Kate, I know I have been too harsh on you, and I am sorry. I have no idea what I am doing here. You were taken from us before we even had a chance at being parents. I am trying." I tell her. She doesn't even look at me.

"Kate, please" I plead with her. She turns her head to look at me, and I can see her eyes all glassy. "I'm sorry I didn't try hard enough to find you. I am sorry you had to go through everything that you have gone through. I wish I could take it all back. I honestly thought you were dead, and I am sorry for that too. But please listen to me, I don't want you dead, and I want you at home with me. Always." I say and wipe away the tears that have fallen down my cheeks.

Katherine follows my movements and wipes her own away. "I just feel that everyone would be better off without me around. Look at the trouble I have caused your club, Dad. If it weren't for me, you'd still have your best friend. If it weren't for me, none of the club girls would have been killed. Everything is my fault" she says between sobs.

I stand up and move towards her bed. Sitting down on the side, I grab hold of her arms and pull her into my chest. "Nothing is your fault. It is the fault of the others who have dared to cross us. We need you, Katherine. You are what brings life to us. Not only does your mother and I need you, but so does that man out there. He has spent every day sitting by your bedside. He even learnt how to help you with moving your legs so your muscles wouldn't die. He loves you" I say to her, kissing her head.

"Can you get Joel please?" Kate asks. I nod my head and untangle my arms from her. I get up and walk to the door, opening it and looking down at Buster. "She wants you," I tell him. I help him up off the floor and move out of the way for him to go in. Buster shuts the door behind himself, and I take Di's hand in mine. "Let's go get some coffee," I say to her, leading her down the hallway.

~~

Joel

I close the door to her room. I don't know what I am feeling right now. I don't know if I am happy she wants to speak to me or sad and angry for the way she yelled at me. All I do know is that my heart is hurting.

I turn around slowly and look at her. Her face is telling me everything I need to know. In quick steps, I make it to her bedside and wrap my arms around her. Kate wraps her arms around my waist and cries into my chest. "I'm so sorry, Joel. Please forgive me" she cries out. I squeeze her tighter to me. "I forgave you the minute I found you" I whisper into her hair.

I can feel Katherine's body, starting to settle. Her sobs are hiccups now. I pull back and notice her eyes are closed. Laying her back on the bed, her eyes open to look at me. "Lay with me" is all she says before her eyes shut.

I kick off my boots and empty my pockets, leaving my stuff on the table beside her bed. I climb in next to her and wrap her in my arms. "I'll always lay with you, Princess" I whisper to her.

Six months later

Kate was discharged from the hospital a week after she attempted suicide. She has mandatory therapy sessions. If she didn't do these, the cops were gonna charge her. Seriously, they were going to charge her. Therapists come and go from the compound daily. All the guys hit on the females until Kate tells them all to get fucked.

We have had couple's sessions, she has had sessions with her parents and sessions with Tracy. Kate looks to be doing much better. She is finally letting everyone in. She is speaking more to us about the way she feels. She isn't closing in on herself anymore. I couldn't be more proud of that woman I call mine.

I know what I have to do, to make sure this woman stays by my side for the rest of my life. As the months go on, I know she is truly the one. She makes me laugh, she makes me smile. She makes me feel things I have never felt before. It is true love, and I wouldn't want to be anywhere else but in her arms.

I find Butch sitting at the bar nursing a whiskey. In his ear, I whisper, "I need a private chat with you" and I walk away heading towards his office. Butch joins me and shuts the door behind us. "What is so important?" he asks me in his gruff voice. "Butch, I love your daughter with every piece of me. I want your blessing to ask her to marry me" I tell him.

The smile that lights up Butch's face makes me smile back. "When do you want to do it?" he asks. "Tonight," I tell him. "Well, let's get this party started" Butch yells out. He claps me on the back, "Welcome to the family, boy" he tells me and walks out of his office.

I follow behind him closely. Taking in everything around me. I drop the smile when I see Katherine. I don't want her knowing what is going to happen. I wrap my arm around her waist and pull her into me, planting a dominant kiss on her lips. "What's gotten into you?" she asks me. "Nothing. Just want to make sure all these fuckers know who you belong to" I tell her with a smirk.

"I belong to myself, first and foremost, Mister," she tells me with her own smirk. I lean down and capture her lips with my own. "I fucking love you," I tell her. "I fucking love you, too," she says and kisses me again. Butch clears his throat and makes the start of a speech. I am too busy looking at Katherine to pay any attention to what he is saying.

"Buster, pay attention to me fuck face," Butch says. I whip my head up quickly and look at him, blushing that I got caught out. "As I was saying, something special is happening at some point tonight, and we will be celebrating until the early hours of tomorrow. I don't know when it's going to happen, but everyone better be on alert" Butch tells the club. All the members cheer loud. A small smile makes its way to my lips.

For the past couple of hours, Butch keeps looking at me with a raised eyebrow. His way of asking me when it is happening. I just keep smiling back at him, shaking my head. Butch approaches me and grabs the back of my cut, pulling me away from the guys. "Come on, Buster. I am hanging out here" he tells me. "Give me 5 minutes. I have to get the ring from my room" I tell him. "Hurry the fuck up, cunt" he says and walks away. I make my way up to my room and find the ring in my bedside table. I open the little box and look at the sparkling diamond. I hope she likes it.

I go back down the stairs and find Katherine, sitting at the bar with her Mum and Tracy. I stand behind her and wrap my hands around her waist, kissing the top of her head. "Hey, baby. What's up?" she asks, looking over her shoulder at me. I drop my arms from her waist and take a step back, bending down on one knee.

Katherine gasps and jumps to her feet. Before I can even open my mouth to ask the question, she has dropped to her knees and is holding me tightly. "Don't ask. The answer is yes" she tells me. I take the ring out of my pocket and slip it onto her left hand's ring finger. "Didn't even have to ask her. SHE SAID YES" I yell the last part out. The room erupts into cheers. The music is turned up even louder.

Everyone comes to congratulate us. Di and Tracy take Katherine with them to fuss over her and the ring. Butch hands me a glass of whiskey. "Cheers," he says. We knock our glasses together and skull the drink back. "Best night of my life, Butch," I tell him. He smiles and pats me on the back.

Kate

The past week has been a whirlwind of different emotions. I cannot wait to call Joel, my husband. He is my soulmate. I just know it.

I want to head into town and go to the bookstore. I haven't been there in a while, and I would like to get a few new books to add to my small collection. "Joel?" I call him. "Yeah, Princess?" he calls back. "Can you take me into town to the bookstore? You can leave me there, and I'll call you to come and get me" I say to him. Joel comes out from the bathroom and nods his head. "Of course, babe," he says.

The ride into town was quick. I climb off his bike and kiss his lips. "I'll call you when I'm done," I tell him and walk into the store. The smell of paper and ink and the old leather covers, makes me feel alive. I browse the aisles at all the books. A few have captured me.

With my back facing the door, I don't see the person entering the store. The last thing I see is John's face as he smiles his evil and nasty yellow rotting teeth smirk. Something is stuck into my neck, and the darkness consumes me quickly after.

Chapter 26- Buried Alive

K ate

John pulls my hair to make me follow him. "Move your fucking arse, whore. Today is the day where your father feels the pain I have felt for the past 24 years" he screams at me. My hands are tied in front of me with cable ties. They are cutting the circulation off in my hands. There is a gag in my mouth to stop me screaming. John drags me out into the middle of the woods. I can see a wooden box in front of me and just behind that is a hole big enough for the box to fit.

I can feel my heart beating through my chest. I know there is only one outcome of this, and it will be my death. John hits me over the head and pushes me into the box. I try to scream through the gag, but it only comes out muffled. "Goodbye, Katherine. Say hello to the fucking devil for me. I will see you there when I die of natural causes. I might even come back there for you and continue our little love affair" John snarls at me.

There is nothing I can do. The lid of the box is nailed on tight. I can feel them push the box into the hole, and I hear the dirt hit the lid. My screams are still muffled. I can't even move my arms to take the gag off. There is no room in the box to move.

This is it for me. The end is here. I never got to experience anything that is worthy of my life. I never got to have children with the man I love. He asked me to marry him only a week ago. How did my life go from, so much happiness to me being buried alive by the man who made me believe he was my father!

I can't hear anything around me now. They must have finished the job and have now left me to rot in this box. I can't breathe. My panic is taking over. My heart rate is through the roof. My lungs are tightening with every breath I try to take—black spots dance in my vision. I close my eyes and say a little prayer in my head.

'Please god if you can hear me, let my family know I loved them dearly and that I am sorry I only got a couple of years with them'. I can now feel my life draining from my body. The darkness is consuming me until there is nothing left.

Joel

Kate has been missing for 12 hours. I know who took her but finding him is going to take a lot of effort. He knows how to hide from us all. We have both computer nerds from both charters trying to track down any movements from John. To see how he got her to where he would have taken her.

I storm into the surveillance room, slamming the door on the wall as I walk in. "Anything yet?" I ask Tracker. "Nope. The only thing I have found was him in town. Where was Kate in the hours before she was taken?" Tracker asks. "She went to the bookstore of all fucking places," I tell him. Tracker moves the camera to the bookstore entrance to see anything. We watch the monitor closely.

"There," Tracker yells and points to the screen. I look even closer and can see the little fucking weasel Brad move in. He never comes out of the front door. Tracker moves to different cameras in the area. Once Brad went into the bookstore, he never came out. Well, that we could see. After a 30 minute window, a blacked-out SUV tears off from the back of the bookstore. "That must have been them," I say to Tracker.

He stops the video and zooms in to get the license plate. "FUCK" he screams. "No fucking plates. Cunts knew what they were doing" he says. Tracker keeps changing cameras to see if he can pick up the car. We know from the footage that they are in an unmarked vehicle heading out of the town. "Where the fuck did the cunt take her?" I say more to myself.

Butch comes rushing in the room. "Josh has been trying to contact me," he tells us. "Did you answer?" I ask him. "Why the fuck would I answer him. He comes in claiming he is my son, leaves me a note telling me he will bring John and Brad to me, but helps in the kidnapping of my fucking daughter. Who the fuck knows where she is now" Butch yells out.

Butch's phone goes off in his pocket again. "Give it to me Butch. I will fucking answer it" I tell him. He throws his phone at me and walks away. "This better be good, Josh," I say as soon as I answer. "I've sent you the location on where Katherine is. I'm telling you now, you better fucking hurry if you want her alive. They have fucking buried her" Josh whispers down the phone. The phone pings in my pocket with a message from Josh. I open the message, and there in front of me is the location where we will find her.

I hang up not saying another word. "Let's go," I say to the boys in the room with me. Running down the hallway into the common room, "Let's roll" I scream out and head towards the clubhouse doors. "Where are we going?" Savage asks. "I have coordinates for Katherine's location. We will need to dig her up. They fucking buried her alive" I tell him.

"Someone bring the truck. We need shovels" Savage yells out. "Let's move fuckers" He calls again. The room is in chaos. Everyone is running towards

the front doors. I have straddled my bike and revved her to life. I just hope
when I have Katherine in my arms, I can do the same for her.

It takes us close to five hours to find the location. We move quickly through
the trees. The location isn't exact, and I am starting to lose my patience.
'FUCKKKKKKKKKKKKKKK" I scream out. We form a human chain
and walk together in a straight line. I hear rustling coming from a tree
beside us and look towards it. I can't see anything, so I break off from the
other guys.

Getting closer to the tree, I see feet sticking out. Hoping they didn't see
me coming, I approach them from behind. As soon as they are my eye
line, I pull my gun out of my cut, turning off the safety and cocking it
back. Pressing the metal against their head, I watch their shoulders slump
in defeat. "Hello, cum bucket. It's been a while" I say in their ear.

"Didn't think you fuckers would find her. Tell me, Buster, how did you
find out about these woods?" Brad says to me. "Don't you worry about
that, Bradley? Just worry about me, holding this gun to your fucking head
and if you don't tell us where the fuck she is, me blowing your tiny little
fucking brains out" I tell him. Pushing him forward with my free hand, we
come out of the bushes together. Butch turns at just the right time.

"Where the fuck is my daughter, Bradley?" Butch yells. "Not fucking telling
you cunt. You will never find her, and when you do, she will be dead. Just
like Jane" Bradley says with malice. "Did you forget that the truth came out
about Jane's death? We never fucking touched her. Your good friend Pete
did it" Butch tells Bradley. Bradley's body freezes in the spot.

"You're fucking lying. Pete didn't kill her. You did!" Brad shouts out.
"Nope, I didn't fucking touch her. I found his little fucking diary when
I finished him off and cleaned out his fucking room. He tied her up and
gutted her. All because he couldn't have her" Butch tells Brad. "Does John
know?" Brad asks. "Well, I sent him the diary. So he fucking should. But

now you will tell us where my fucking daughter is before Buster there blows your fucking brains out" Butch demands.

"Walk another 500 meters through those trees, and you will find the disturbed dirt," Brad tells us. Savage leads a group of guys forward to make sure we were being told the truth. "GOT IT. DIG YOU MOTHER-FUCKERS" we hear Savage yell out. I hit Brad over the back of his head with the butt of my gun, ultimately knocking the fucker out.

Leaving his body on the ground, I run towards where the rest of them are. They are still digging trying to get to the box. "Fuck, I found something" Savage calls out. I run over to him and see the corner of a wooden box. "Hurry and let's get this out of the ground" I yell out. Using my bare hands, I start digging the dirt away from the box.

After another 20 minutes of moving the dirt, we have finally cleared the top of the box off. "Fuck!" I say. "it's nailed on," I tell them. Savage hands me a shovel. "Get that under the lip, and we will all push down together," he tells me. I do as he said, and on the count of three, we push the shovel down. It lifts the nail clean out of its spot. Moving around to all the nails, we do the same thing.

Once the box was open, my breath catches in my throat. My Princess lays there—a gag in her mouth and cable ties on her wrists. My heart breaks at the sight of my beauty. Picking her up, she feels limp and cold. I rest my head on her chest and can hear a faint heartbeat. Laying her on the ground, I remove the gag from her mouth and start talking to her.

"Princess, it's me. Come back to me, please. I need you. I need you so fucking badly baby" I whisper in her ear. Butch kneels beside us and places his head on her chest. "We have a faint heartbeat. DOC WHAT DO WE DO?" Butch yells to Doc. "Well first things first Butch, get the fuck out of my fucking way," Doc tells him.

Butch stands up and rests his hand on my shoulder. I shake my head. I am not moving from my spot. This is my woman, and if Doc tries to tell me to move, I will punch him in the fucking face. Doc starts working on Katherine. As much as he could in this environment. "Someone bring the fucking truck up here. I need to get her back to the clubhouse to set her up on the monitors" Doc yells out.

Three of the guys head off to get the truck. Doc checks Katherine's pulse and her breathing. He keeps shaking his head. "Doc?" I question him with my eyes. "If we can get her back quickly Buster, I have a chance at saving her. Right now it doesn't look too good" he tells me with sorrow in his eyes. I can feel the tears forming in my own eyes. I can't lose her.

"Butch" I call for him. "Yeah?" he asks me. "You better find that brother of yours. I am going to be the one who fucking guts him like a fish" I tell Butch with anger in my voice. He has nearly killed my Princess. If she dies, he will die a more painful fucking death. Long and slow torture. I'll have him watch us kill his stupid whore of a wife and her stupid fucking cunt of a son. Then it'll be John's turn. Long and slow. The more painful, the better.

As soon as Kate was loaded in the truck, the truck was gone. We all moved back towards our bikes. Picking up our little friend along the way. "Tie him to the back of my bike, and I will drag him all the way back to the clubhouse," Butch tells us. Tying Brad to the back of Butch's bike was the highlight of the day. If this doesn't kill him, at least he will be in pain.

Getting back to the clubhouse. Brad was barely holding onto life. Butch opened the shed door, and we all know what was going to happen. "String him up by his ankles," Butch says. The prospects got to work, doing as they were told. "Once he is up, leave him. I will deal with him when I am ready" Butch says. The prospects nod and finish up what they need to do.

Butch and I enter the clubhouse and head straight down to Doc. Opening the door, there is my Princess laying on the bed. She is hooked up to every machine possible. Her heart rate is slowly picking up. Her breathing is starting to return to normal. "Guys, she is still in a bad way. I have her on fluids right now. There is nothing else I can do. She needs to fight this" Doc says to us. Both Butch and I nod our heads. "I'll give you a few minutes with her, but I need you guys to give her space too," Doc tells us and leaves the room.

Butch goes over to Kate first. "Hey, Princess. I need you to get better, okay. You have a lot of life to discover and a wedding to plan. We need you to come back to us, okay. I love you, Kate" Butch kisses her on the forehead, walks over to me and pats me on the shoulder. Leaving the room, he takes one more look at her, then shuts the door behind him.

I finally let my tears fall at the sight of my girl. My heart is breaking seeing her like this. Not knowing if she will come back from this is killing me. "Come on, baby. I need you. Please, Kate. Don't leave me" I whisper into her ear. I pick up her hand and give her a small kiss on her knuckles. "Please come back to me" I whisper again, letting my tears fall down onto her hand.

Placing her hand back onto the bed. I slowly get up from the chair and kiss her forehead. "I love you" I whisper onto her lips and place a small kiss on them. I stand up straight and wipe my eyes. Leaving the room, I take one more look at her. I just hope and pray that she will come back to me soon.

Chapter 27- The beginning of the end

J oel

The only mission this club has is to kill John and Brad. Brad is on the brink of death as it is. They have ruined Katherine. She is still unconscious, and it has been a week. The doctors are not hopeful. She's laying dying in that hospital bed. Butch and Diana are not coping. The club is going mad.

Doc told us the day after we found her, that, she needed a hospital. He couldn't do everything for her, so that is what we did. We sent her to the local hospital and have left guards on her. She is my fucking world, and I will not let that cunt get his grubby fingers on her again.

Bones and Danger are both out looking for John. The cunt has gone into hiding. It is probably the smartest thing he could do, but I swear that it will be a long, slow and painful death when we find him. He has fucked with us one too many times.

"Word from Bones is that John is back in town. Boys are following" Savage yells out. "Everyone get ready" Butch yells, kissing Diana on the head. "It's time to finish this," I say to myself. Running out of the clubhouse to my bike.

Butch takes the lead, Savage and I ride behind him, and the rest of the club is behind us. The ride to Castlemain is long and tiring. We only stop to piss, and that's it. The wind is harsh, and the rain has started. We keep going. It is time to get John and string him up by his fucking ankles. He has nearly killed my woman twice now.

Pulling into Castlemain, what should have taken two days only took us one. We pull up into Bones' compound, parking our bikes and climbing off them one by one. Bones greats us from the porch. "Welcome boys. Come on in and let's get the party started" Bones calls out to all of us. We look at him in confusion.

"Why are we having a party?" I ask him. "I got a surprise for you all. So, come in, and I'll show you it" Bones replies. Butch walks in first followed by Savage and the rest of the guys. I hang back and wait. I don't really want to party. My Katherine is laying in a hospital bed, on the brink of death. I should be there with her and not here drinking and laughing and having fun.

I finally go inside the clubhouse. The room is packed with men and women, drinking and cheering. I watch as Butch approaches me with a look in his eyes that I don't understand. "Come on. We have to go into the basement for our surprise" he says to me, with sarcasm dripping from his voice. I follow Butch when he turns and walks away.

Walking down the basement stairs, I hold my breath. Nothing good comes from down here. All the men who have lost their lives down here for double-crossing us. Making it into the centre of the darkroom, a small light leading our way. I am standing right behind Butch and Savage when the lights get turned on.

Sitting in a chair in the middle of the room is a bloody and beaten John. He looks up as the lights are turned on. The look in his eyes of pure shock and then anger. "Fuck off. You can't do anything to me. You kill me and then Brad will come after you" John spits out at Butch.

"Funny you mention Brad. He won't be hurting anyone from now on, John" Butch tells his brother. John looks confused at Butch's answer. "To clear it up, John. Brad is hanging out in my shed, literally hanging by his feet. He is probably dead by now" Butch says with a shrug of his shoulders. "Don't lie to me, Baxter. You don't have Brad. He was standing guard, making sure no one got to your dead daughter" John spits out.

"That is where you are wrong, yet again little brother. You see, I have a spy amongst you. Someone told me what was happening to my Princess, and we could save her before she died. When we found the location, Brad was there, and after a few minutes of roughing him up, we had Katherine out of the hole she was in" Butch says with a smirk.

I have my own smirk on my face, knowing that John is about to die, and I am looking forward to watching every minute of his demise. My phone pings in my pocket, I pull it out and read the message. My heart rate picks up, and I can't help the laugh that comes from my throat. Butch turns to look at me with one of his eyebrows raised.

I turn my phone to him to show him the message. The tears start to form in his eyes, leaving him with a glassy look. "John, you are a piece of scum. Not worth anything in this life. You see, that was my wife who messaged Buster here. She was informing us that Katherine has woken up from her little sleep. You thought you would beat us, but at the end of the day, I was stronger. I waited and waited patiently for you to fuck up" Butch tells him.

John pisses his pants at Butch's words. "You can't do shit to me" John yells out. "Really?" Butch questions him. "You are weak, Baxter. You will never hurt me because I am blood" John tries to reason with Butch. "I am going to have great pleasure in watching the life drain out of your eyes, John. You are not blood to me. Blood doesn't kidnap and hurt their own family members. You fucked up taking my daughter from me" Butch yells at him.

"You took Jane from me" John replies. "I never fucking touched Jane. That was Raider. He was the one who killed her and then allowed my club to carry the blame. You are sick and twisted. You worked alongside the guy who murdered your woman for years and didn't even know, so stop trying to blame it on me." Butch yells. He turns his back and walks out of the basement.

I approach John and punch him in the jaw. "That there cunt, is for all the hurt you put my woman through" I yell at him. Punching him again in the face, "That's for me" I tell him. Turning around, I walk out of the basement with Savage in toe. Getting up to the common room, Butch is sitting at the bar, sinking back a glass of whiskey.

"Tell them Buster" Butch yells out. "Katherine is awake. She remembers everything that happened, and she is waiting for us to come home with that piece of shit. She wants to help end him" I yell out to the room. The hooting and hollering from the members could be heard from outer space.

The party doesn't last too much longer. Butch's crew are ready to ride back and take John to his final resting place. Of course, we need to kill him first. We load up the van with a bruised and unconscious John, and the rest of us jump on our bikes. "Don't worry about speed limits boys. Let's get back to the clubhouse" Butch yells out over the sounds of bikes revving.

"Hang on, Kate. I'm coming home to you."

~~

Kate

I wake up alone in a hospital room. I have wires attached to my chest and an I.V running up my arm. I cough to get someone's attention. I open my mouth to speak, but my throat is hurting. It is dry, and I cough again. Choking on air. The door to the room opens, and I come face to face with Mum. "Holy shit baby girl" she cries out. Running over to my bed and pulling me into her arms.

I am crying alongside her. Mum is rubbing my back and kissing my cheek. "I'm so happy you are awake, Katherine. We were all so worried about you" Mum says to me. I look over to the water jug that is on the table next to my bed. I point my finger towards it and Mum quickly pours me a cup.

I gulp the water down quickly. Feeling the coolness of the water instantly lubricate my throat. "Thank you" I whisper to her. Mum smiles back at me. "Where's Joel?" I ask her on a whisper. "Oh, they had some news. They have gone out of town" Mum tells me. "Phone?" I ask. Mum hands me her phone, and I open up the messages.

Hey baby, It's Katherine. Please come back now. I need you next to me. If you have found John and Brad, I want to help get rid of them. Do not have any fun without me. I love you!!!!

I send the message to Joel's phone. I don't hear anything back from him. I lay down and look at Mum. She has the biggest smile on her face, just staring back at me. I pat the bed next to me for Mum, and she lays down next to me. Holding me close to her.

I don't know how long Mum and I had slept for, but it was the best sleep of my life. I have my Mum. My real Mum. The one who carried me and birthed me. The one who lost me to kidnapping. The one who now has me again and will never let anything happen to me.

The doctor walks in the room and smiles when he sees me awake. "Good to have you back, Katherine," he says. He does a few checks on me. "I think you could probably be discharged later today or even tomorrow morning. Everything looks good" he says with a smile. I smile back at him. "Thank you. I would rather get out of here today, though. I will recover better at home" I tell him. He nods his head and leaves the room.

"Hey, Mum?" I call. "Yeah, babe?" Mum questions. "Have you heard from Dad or Joel? I sent Joel a message and never heard back from him" I tell her. I don't want to start crying, but I can feel the tears fill my eyes. "I spoke with your Dad after you fell asleep last night. They were on their way back from Castlemain. They should be back soon" she tells me.

A few hours pass and the doctor comes back in the room with some papers in his hands. "Here are your discharge papers, Katherine. Just sign where I have left a cross, and you will be free to go" he says. I take the papers and pen and sign my name away. Handing everything back to him, he leaves the room. I get up and grab the clothes that Mum had laid out on my bed.

I have a quick shower and get dressed. Leaving the hospital room, I walk down the quiet hallway. I press the button for the elevator and wait for the door to open. Once they do, I spot the most delicious looking man I have ever seen in my life.

"Hey, baby," he says to me. I jump into his arms, pressing my lips to his. Joel stumbles back a bit but catches himself. "I've missed you, Princess," Joel says on my lips. "I missed you" I whisper back. "How did you find me?" I ask him. He places me back on my feet. "I want to tell you, but your Dad told me to wait until you were home. So that we could all talk to you together" he says to me. I smile at his answer and wrap my arms around his body, resting my head on his chest.

Joel gets us back to the clubhouse in no time. Walking through the front doors, I feel a weight being lifted off my shoulders. Everyone is here. All the members are cheering that I am back, and I can feel the love from all of them. I see my Dad first and walk straight into his arms. He wraps me up tight. "I'm so happy to see you," he tells me. I look up at his face and see the love he has for me, shining in his eyes.

"I'm so happy to see you too, Dad. I've missed you" I tell him, resting my head on his chest. "Princess, we need to talk," Dad says to me. Everyone in the room goes quiet. I step back from Dad's embrace, instantly feeling the cold air. "We have a surprise for you. Would you like to see it?" Dad asks me. I nod my head at him with a big smile on my face.

Dad walks me out of the clubhouse, down towards the shed. "Close your eyes, Princess" Dad tells me. I close my eyes, and a blindfold is then placed over them. Two people grab onto my arms and walk me into the shed. Muffled noises are coming from the main floor. "Can I take it off yet?" I ask. "In a minute, Princess" Dad tells me.

I wait until I am told to remove the blindfold, and once I do, an evil smirk crosses my face.

"Hello, Uncle John. Did you miss me?"

Who is ready for what's to come? Hold onto your hats people. The fun begins in the next chapter!

Chapter 28- The end is here

This chapter depicts violent scenes. Please read at your own discretion.

Kate

I look at John. He is hanging upside down in the shed. "Shocked to see me alive?" I ask him, taunting him for a reaction. "Remove the gag," I say to the boys. Two prospects run up and remove the gag from John's mouth. I stand back waiting for him to react to me.

"They got to you in time?" John says. I just stand there staring at him. "Clearly. I'm standing here, aren't I?" I question back. He scoffs. "How did they find you?" he asks. I look to Dad for the answer. "I can do one better" I hear the voice and watch as he steps through the shed door.

I gasp as I watch Josh walk in. He has a smile on his face that makes his features stand out. Just in this light, I can see Dad in him. "YOU" John spits out. "What you thought I was gonna go against my family? If you seriously thought that, you are one fucked up person" Josh says to him with a massive smile still planted on his face.

Dad stands next to Josh and wraps an arm around his shoulders. "You thought that you could weasel your way into his life and make him hate us. The day you told him about me was the day I got my son back. You fucked up John, and I for one cannot wait to watch what Kate and Buster do to you" Dad tells him, his smirk getting wider and wider.

I look behind John and see another body hanging from the roof. "Is that Brad?" I ask. Dad nods his head at me. I walk around John, approaching Brad's hanging body. "Oh, he is already dead," I say out loud. "Damn, I was looking forward to playing with him," I tell the boys. I kick Brad in the head and watch his body swing from the chains.

Going back to the front of the room, I grab the boning knife off the table. "I have the perfect plan for this," I say, causing the boys to all take a step back. I walk around over to Brad's lifeless body, stabbing the knife straight into his dick. "Do you need a new gag for John?" I ask Dad. I look at Dad, and he stares straight back at me. Raising my eyebrow Dad then realises what I am thinking.

Dad cringes and then nods his head. I get to work, making a new gag for John. I finish my masterpiece and move back towards the hanging John. "Any last words, John?" I ask him. I have the gag hidden behind my back so he couldn't see what I had planned. "Fuck you, you little whore. No one will love you. You are damaged beyond repair, and no one will want a used up whore like you" John spits out. I look at Buster and can see the steam coming out of his ears.

"That is where you are wrong, John. You see, I have finally found who I am. I have a whole club here who loves me and a man that can't wait to marry me. You are the one that is damaged and used up. But enough talking. It's time for you to fuck off" I say to him. I look at the prospects, "Pick up his head and hold it still" I tell them. They move quickly to do as I have said.

I get closer to his face. John is clenching his jaw; he must sense I have a fucked up mind. "We can do this the easy way John and that is where you just open your mouth and take what I am giving you, or, we can do it the hard way. That is where I smash your fucking jaw to pieces, shove the gag down it and then tape your bottom jaw up. You choose?" I tell him.

I count down from ten for his answer. When I get to three, he opens his mouth to say something, but I am quicker. I shove Brad's dick and balls into his mouth and as far as I can get it down the back of his throat. John starts choking on them, trying to spit them out. "Alright boys, playtime is over. Let's end this good for nothing piece of shit's life" I yell out.

Joel stands beside me and holds my hand. "You ready for this Princess?" he asks me. I look into his eyes, and I can see all the love he has for me shining in them. I lean up and kiss his lips. "I was born ready for this," I tell him. Joel moves to stand behind me, I pick up the knife, and he puts his hand on top of mine.

Working as a team, we start the gutting process. Blood is flying everywhere. We don't do a straight cut. Zig zagging from John's pelvis, through his abdomen and down his chest. Getting to his neck, Joel and I start a sawing action. Wendy had to suffer at the hands of this man, and now we are repaying the favour.

We cut all the flesh and muscle from around his neck. Leaving him hanging upside down, draining the life and blood out of him. "Josh?" I call for my new brother. "Yeah, Katherine?" he asks. "Seeing as this piece of shit, killed your mother. Would you like to do the final thing to him?" I ask. Josh looks at me, confused. "Kick his motherfucking head off" I yell out.

Josh smiles and steps forward. "I would be honoured," he says. I step back and give him room. "I know you are already dead you cunt, but this is for all the times you lied to me. This is for all the times I had to watch you hurt my sister, and this is for my mother" he yells at John's dead body. Josh walks back a couple of steps and lining up his shot. He moves quickly, and we watch John's head bounce off the shed wall. Cheers from the boys are deafening in this small room.

We all walk outside to Mum. She has the hose ready to wash us down. Joel and I stand under the spray of the hose. Mum looks at me, drops the hose then pulls me into her arms. "It's over now, Princess. It's over now" she whispers into my hair. I hold onto her tighter and let the tears fall.

All the members are standing around, watching Mum and me in our embrace. "Move along boys. There is nothing to see here" Dad calls out. All of the guys move into the clubhouse, yelling and cheering that the end of John had come. We all know now that life will get back to its normalness. Well as normal as a motorcycle club can be.

Mum and I finally let each other go, I am then pulled into my Dad's arms. He holds me tighter to him than Mum did. "I'm proud of you, Princess. You have shown us that you are not afraid to get your hands dirty and you have beaten your demons. We, your Mum and I are happy that you are still here with us and we will never let you go" Dad says to me. I can feel the tears still slipping down my cheeks.

"I love you, Dad" I whisper to him. "I love you, too, Princess" he whispers back. He steps back from the hug, holding me at arm's length. "Get inside and wash this dirty blood off you. We have a party to be at" Dad says. I smile at him and take Joel's hand in mine. "Let's shower and then get this party started," I say to him.

Joel follows me up the stairs, pinching my bum every chance he gets. I swat his hands away each and every time. "Listen here, Buster. You keep doing that, and you will be showering alone" I tell him with a stern voice. Joel picks me up and throws me over his shoulder and races up the rest of the stairs. "No way, I'm getting my woman in the shower to do other things than just cleaning," he says with a hint of lust in his voice.

I giggle as he throws my bedroom door open and kicks it closed with his foot. Joel places me down on the bed, locks the bedroom door and starts stripping out of his clothes. "Listen here, Katherine. I have gone days without being inside of you, you have one minute to get naked, and in that shower, otherwise, I will take you here. Blood, guts and all." Joel says to me.

I do as I am told and get as naked as the day I was born. I run into the bathroom and turning on the water. Joel comes in from behind me, pushing me under the water. "Fuck, it's cold" I yell out. I quickly turn the hot water tap on to get the water warm. Joel starts kissing my neck and pushing me into the tiles.

"Babe, you need to stick it in me now; otherwise you will have to use your hand," I tell him. Joel grabs my hips pulling them, so I arch my back. Without warning, he rams his cock inside of me. I moan loud, encouraging him to keep going. Joel keeps his hard and fast rhythm, bringing me closer and closer to my orgasm. "You better cum now, Princess" he whispers into my ear.

I move one of my hands down to my clit, rubbing it faster and faster. My orgasm washes over me, and I scream out my release. Joel grunts out his own, wrapping his arms around my waist, pulling me up straighter against his chest. "Fuck, I love you" he whispers into my ear. I feel his member fall out of me, and I turn around in his arms.

"I love you, too," I tell him, kissing his lips. We quickly finish off washing our bodies in the shower. Getting dressed was another challenge. An hour later, we finally make it down the stairs to the party. "What took you fuckers so long to get down here?" Savage calls out. "Exactly that. We were fucking" I tell him. The room erupts into laughter, and Joel and I join in.

I walk straight to the bar and grab a whiskey that Tracy pours for me. "Good to see you so happy, gorgeous girl," she says to me. I lean over the bar and grab the front of her shirt. Pressing my lips to hers. "I used to think you made a mistake saving me, but now I see the bigger picture, and I thank you," I tell her. The look of shock on her face after I kissed her made me giggle.

"Oi, I told you if there was going to be any girl on girl action, I wanted in," Savage says coming up behind me. "That's all your getting, Sav. I love Tracy, but I prefer cock and balls" I tell him with a wink. He laughs, walking around the bar to kiss his woman.

"Can I have everyone's attention" my Dad calls out. The music stops, and the chatter quietens down. "The members and I had a vote. We had to choose who was going to be my VP. We all voted, and it was voted that Savage is the new VP" Dad calls out. All the guys start cheering again. Savage looked like he was gonna cry.

"But, With Savage as the VP, I needed a new S.A.A. Boys, let's hear it for Buster. The new Sergeant-At-Arms is my soon to be son-in-law Buster. The room erupts again into cheers and whistling. I turn around and watch my man walk up and get his new patch. Both of the guys shake Dad's hand. The smiles could not be wiped from their faces, ever!

The night went on with drinking and dancing and a whole lot of shenani-gans. A weight had been lifted from my shoulders. Life for me now is only going to get better. I do not have to worry about John or Brad. I have gained a whole new family and a new brother. Josh still seemed out of place, but none of the guys here made him feel unwanted.

"Josh" I call him. He looks up at me and gives me a small smile. "I forgive you," I tell him, wrapping my arms around him. He tenses under my arms and then relaxes, wrapping his arms around me. "I don't deserve your forgiveness, Katherine," he tells me. "You didn't know the truth, and you helped these guys rescue me. Yeah, it might have taken a while, but you did it. You saved me" I tell him.

"Thank you, brother," I say to him.

Chapter 29- Epilogue

Kate

Ten years ago, I ran away from people who I thought were my parents. I ran away from their abuse and found out the truth. I found out I was kidnapped as a baby, all because my father who I found out later was my uncle, first partner was murdered, and the blame fell on my birth parents.

My birth parents were innocent this whole time, and my uncle wanted revenge. He abused me, tortured me, raped me, and tried to kill me on numerous occasions, but I am still here at the end of the day. I am still breathing and loving life.

Six years ago, I met my now-husband. Yes, our beginning wasn't smooth sailing, with thanks to my selfish behaviour, but he never left me. He always stood beside me and believed that I could become a better person with a life full of love and care. Something I never got growing up.

I'm sitting at the picnic table in the compound watching the boys having running races, rubbing my swollen eight-month pregnant belly. Things have been amazing for all of us.

Buster and I got married a year after killing John. We waited to have kids. He wanted to make sure I was really ready for it, and well look where we are now. Our first baby is on the way. We decided against finding out the sex. We wanted a little surprise.

Savage and Tracy tied the knot a year ago. She was already knocked up by the time they got married, and they welcomed a beautiful little Princess of their own, four months later. Little Riley is gorgeous and has everyone wrapped around her little finger. She is about to turn one and is the life of the party. I feel sorry for Tracy.

Josh found his place here with the crew. He was welcomed in with open arms in the end. He helped save me from John and Brad. He started dating one of the men's daughters, and they have been going strong ever since. He asked me how to go about proposing to her. I slapped him, kissed his cheek and told him to just do it. Fingers crossed it happens today.

Mum and Dad. Wow. They have been through so much shit together and have come out stronger. They are still madly in love. They welcomed Josh into the family. They always tell him that they owe him. Josh being Josh, brushes it off like normal. Mum and Dad are more in love today than they were yesterday.

This right here. This is what I had been craving all my life. This connection, this family, just this!

I stand up from my chair; the pain in my back is making me uncomfortable. I have had back pain for the past couple of days but ignored it. Just thinking it was normal. This baby is fucking huge. I walk three steps and have to stop. "Joel, I just pissed my pants" I yell out. The boy's all start laughing. Beer and whiskey being spat everywhere.

Joel stands beside me "I don't think that is your piss babe. I think this baby is coming" he tells me. "Ohhhh that would explain the back pain then," I say to him. He looks at me with concern in his eyes. "How long have you had back pain?" he asks. "Couple of days. Nothing I couldn't handle though" I say to him. Kissing his cheek, I start moving towards the clubhouse.

I climb up two steps and have to stop as a pushing feeling rushes over my body. "OH FUCK" I scream out. Joel runs up beside me, "What's wrong?" he asks. "I don't think we will make it to a hospital. Get me into Doc" I yell at him through gritted teeth. Joel picks me up and carries me down to Doc. Kicking the door open with his foot.

"DOC" He yells out. "What now?" Doc questions us. I start removing my pants and undies and climb up on the bed. "Get this devil out of me" I cry out. Doc grabs his gloves and puts them on. Joel growls at Doc looking up my snatch. "You want me to deliver your child, Buster?" he asks Joel. Joel nods his head and whispers 'yes' to him. "Good. Shut the fuck up. Hold your woman's hand and let me do what I am fucking trained to do" Doc yells at him.

Three pushes later, and I can feel the baby's head pop out of me. I can't see what Doc is doing, but I have my full faith in him to deliver my baby. "Katherine, when I tell you, I need you to give me one last big push. Okay?" Doc says to me. "Mmhmmm" I reply. I have no words right now. "Now," Doc says. I bare down and give him one final big push.

I open my eyes when I hear the shrill cry of a baby being placed on my chest. I open my eyes to look at my child. "I have a fucking son" Joel cries out. I look down at the baby and move the legs to have a look myself. There in front of me was my son's junk. I cry tears of joy and happiness. I have a son.

Joel kisses my head and then kisses the babies. He goes down to Doc and kisses him too. I watch as my husband runs out of the room into the common room screaming. "I HAVE A SON. I HAVE A SON." I listen to my husband, and his excitement rubs off onto me.

Holding my baby and looking into his eyes, I make him a promise that I intend to keep.

"From this day forward, I promise to always hold you close to me. I promise to never let you go through what I have had to go through, and I promise that everyone in this house will love you until their final breaths. You are a light to shine brightly from now until forever."

The End

www.ingramcontent.com/pod-product-compliance
Lightning Source LLC
Chambersburg PA
CBHW070355200726
48294CB00003B/921